A saga of space travel, revenge and a
really cool rocking horse

Time Warp

Book One

WILLIAM PAUL LAZARUS

WolfSinger Publications   Security, Colorado

I

Bathed in the light of a universe of stars, Dalian Crown Prince Anton leaned back in the plush captain's chair and watched the panorama of space. Isolated, hurtling through the cosmos, he finally began to relax. The awful events that sent him into space seemed so far behind him now: the civil war with neighboring Kajia, the attack on Dalia, the decision to send him to safety with only Thurgose, his automatonic horse, for a companion. There had been no time for anyone else to accompany him.

Out here, on the swirling edge of the galaxy, Anton felt such calmness. He could have picked up one of his 4-D video games, but did not. For a moment, he could be lazy, resting between lessons from Thurgose. He gazed languidly at the starry blackness, munching on freeze-dried dydala. He thought about having some humsta, the syrupy porridge that was his normal breakfast, but was mostly grateful that choosing what to eat was the hardest decision he now had to make.

"Brubiscon," Thurgose interrupted in its metallic voice.

Anton turned his head. As usual, the little horse was hooked into the controls. However, it had shifted to the side, hooking its legs into the media control unit.

Tossing his blond hair in disgust, Anton waved it off. "I don't want to see a movie," he said. "I just want to enjoy the view." He turned sideways to stretch his short legs across the chair, letting his bare feet dangle over the armrest.

Thurgose did not respond, but simply dimmed the interior lights and projected a holographic image against the far wall. Anton gasped and sat up as his father, Frighem Laren of Dalia and Kajia appeared. He looked so real Anton almost reached out a hand to touch his father, whose face had become a purple mask as age seeped through the familiar yellow coloring of youth.

To Anton's surprise, the Frighem had smeared chocolate-colored culka powder under his eyes. Only fighters on Dalia wore that since it spoke of determination and death. Anton leaned forward in his seat.

"My son," the Frighem said in hushed tones. "When you see this, I may be dead." He began talking about the civil war between his planet and the neighboring planet Kajia when the old man suddenly grew silent. His mouth remained open, and his lips moved, but no words came out. Anton glanced quickly at Thurgose, the robotic rocking horse projecting the video, and back at the wall. His father seemed unaware of the loss of sound.

Then, strangely, a hole appeared in the Frighem's forehead, blossoming red and ugly in the middle of one of the deep purple creases. His eyes seemed to roll upward then disappear. In a moment, the picture vanished, too, swallowed by the darkness of the room.

Anton gasped. Stunned, he realized he had seen the assassination of his father. His stomach heaved. He slowly began to cry as the lights went on. Death did not usually move him; on a planet where life spans were short, death happened frequently. However, as prince, Anton had one clear duty: to perform the funeral rituals for his father. Far away, he was not there to say the Mourning Prayer, to light the traditional pile candle. He could not dust his father's hands and feet with the good Dalian dirt.

After a moment, Anton collected himself. In his precarious position, isolated in space, he could not grieve long. He ran a hand through his lavender hair and allowed his natural yellow hue to return to his face. A couple of tears crossed his black eyes, but that was all.

He took a deep breath. He would be strong. He had to be.

He started to stand. There was a lot to think about.

"Please remain seated," Thurgose said. "There is more."

Somewhat uneasy, Anton dropped back into his chair, turning again to face the wall. The light from Thurgose's plastic eyes shone again, but no image appeared. Instead, there was a loud buzz followed by a calm, harsh, sinister male voice.

"Anton," it said. "I am going to kill you." Anton sat up, trying to recognize the voice. It had an odd accent, but he had heard it before.

The speaker continued with calm invective. "You can run to the outer reaches of the universe." His voice was youthful, vibrant and arrogant. "I will find out. I...." There was a harsh sound, and the tape cut off, too.

"What is all that?" Anton cried, jumping to his feet. He wanted to do something, anything, but didn't know what. Thurgose was as impassive as usual. It stood by the controls, slowly shifting its legs back and forth to activate the various functions. Anton heard a click. The interior lights returned to the normal level. Everything seemed the way it was before, except nothing was the same.

Thurgose rocked back, disengaged itself from the controls and rolled to Anton's side. "I am your protector," it intoned. "I have been programmed to insulate you against bodily harm."

Anton trembled and touched the plastic head, finding the special sensor device built into the automaton's surface that sent reassuring warmth into his hand. The automaton came to his waist, the perfect height for petting without reaching.

"Do you know who was threatening me?" Anton asked.

"Yes." The horse paused. "I have analyzed the voice, and it belongs to Wyron, the Prince of Kajia."

Anton nodded grimly. He should have known. As royal children, they had often played together. Now, Wyron wanted control of the two sister planets. Almost unconsciously, Anton continued to stroke the horse's head.

"I wonder where he is now," he thought aloud.

"I have detected no metallic compounds or radiation in the vicinity," Thurgose reported. "The exterior sensing equipment has been activated since we left Dalia, and no such signals have been received. I monitor them on a regular basis. You may be assured of your safety."

Anton relaxed a little. He walked over to the closest portal. He pressed the switch, and the blue metal shield swung wide. Looking out, he could see the bands of stars stretching in all directions. Not a few minutes ago, everything seemed so calm and inviting. Now, there seemed no pattern, no clear paths.

"Where are we going?" he asked Thurgose. He didn't expect an answer and didn't get one. Thurgose simply ran through a rainbow of colors as if searching memory banks for a response it knew didn't exist.

"Did you have to show me that today?" Anton continued. He could have enjoyed a few more moments of peace. That illusion was gone forever.

"I can only do as programmed," Thurgose said.

"That's all I can do, too," Anton replied. He felt very depressed. All he really knew was confined to the metallic interior of this ship.

His memories were a mishmash of images that floated together in a hazy soup. His father was dead; his planet lay in desolate, contaminated ruins. And he floated in space toward some unknown target. Somewhere out there, perhaps a few light years behind, rode someone who wanted to kill him. Anton turned back and looked at Thurgose.

"I am the Frighem now," he said almost in wonder. The very idea awed him.

"Yes," Thurgose said. "You are chief flower among the eastern skies, god of youth and firmament, first son of the great Frighem Laren, son of the great queen Rena, Brubiscon of the Gorean festival and bearer of the Whiten bushels at the festival of Alain. And, you are also the Frighem."

Anton shook his head. What did any of those titles mean on a spaceship somewhere in deep space? "I am the leader of one," he noted sourly.

"I am ever ready to obey my Brubiscon," Thurgose assured him.

"Then what am I supposed to do now?" Anton asked.

"Now is everything," Thurgose recited. "Dugozy. 1654."

"No philosophy," Anton pleaded. "My head is reeling."

Thurgose responded by changing from a slight yellow color to an off-gray, the signal it was ready to instruct, and began to roll along the metallic strips in the flooring to the teaching nook.

Sad and disheartened, Anton followed the little automaton into the aisle. And, for just a moment, he tried to ignore what fully he realized lay ahead.

II

Anton checked himself in the mirror, something he rarely did, and was surprised to see his face had changed. It was just as round with a nub for a nose and vertical lips. Dark eyes looked back at him with their usually silver iris. However, his usual pale yellow color was now grayer. His chin seemed to have grown the darkest with the line of color stretching toward his ear holes on both sides. Puzzled, he rubbed the graying skin and felt a roughness. He knew instantly what was wrong: scrofula, the dread disease that often killed or maimed his countrymen. This was the way Dalia's last hope would end his days, slowly being eaten away by the awful illness.

He staggered back against the wall.

Alerted by the thump, Thurgose appeared and curiously nuzzled the teenager's leg.

"It's over, Thurgose. It's over," Anton moaned. He sighed and turned up his eyes in sadness.

The animal considered that. "What is, Brubiscon?" Thurgose was clearly puzzled by the lack of any obvious cause for distress. Already alert to danger, it had activated surveillance wires near its ears and had turned a defensive brown.

"I think I am dying," Anton mumbled. He straightened and looked into the mirror again. The scofula consisted of small, dark splotches. He had never seen an example close up before. It looked horrid.

Thurgose immediately ran a sensor from its mouth to Anton's leg. "All vital signs continue normal," it reported.

"Can't you see what's on my face?" Anton whirled and cried. "You stupid grocka." He caught himself instantly before adding new insults. "Oh, how would you know," he muttered. "You can't get it. Look at my chin." He bent over. "Look. See for yourself."

"Ah," Thurgose said solemnly, "I perceive the situation. And I can affect a cure." He turned and rolled away. Anton gaped. Had his father thought of even a remedy for scofula? Perhaps there had been only enough serum for one. That must be why no one else had been treated. He took a deep breath as Thurgose returned, carrying something on the platform between its legs.

"I present this to you," it said. Anton was sure he could hear humor in the horse's voice. That wasn't possible, he thought as he bent over. There was a razor there.

"I'm supposed to scrape it off?" he asked.

Thurgose nodded. "That is what one does with a beard," it said.

Anton had nothing to say after that, but the story was carefully added to the video log of the trip. It gave them a something to laugh about amid the steady gloom.

Lost in thought, but clean shaven, Anton devoted most of his time to playing 4-D video games. During his latest session, he had managed to shoot down 22,000 points worth of enemy aircraft. While that was an impressive total, he was still a long way from his high level mark. He played almost mechanically now, aware what would happen on the game board and responding to it.

He also had taken to wearing his adult nuvras. As Frighem, even with no one to rule but a robot, he must be an adult now.

His feet were visible through the crossed leather top; his heels were thrust out the back. Only men could wear such shoes. Only they were brave enough to withstand Dalia's harsh, crusty soil with almost bare feet. Young feet must be protected. An adult had scars to prove his masculinity. Women, too, wore special open-toed shoes when they were of age to demonstrate their strength and courage.

Flushed with excitement, Anton had taken his first steps in the nuvras. They felt odd. Now, they were commonplace even if they did not reveal any scars on his bare feet. He regretted the missing signs of maturity. All grown men had scars on their feet. His only scars came where the thongs cut into his arches. He endured the pain proudly, hoping someday, the scars would stretch to the sides so the people he would meet when he landed would realize they were confronting an adult.

Thurgose rolled to his side and watched for a moment as Anton zapped another dozen ships with a flick of his wrist. "Now is the time," the animal announced.

Anton protested. He shifted his attention for a moment, and his own video ship suddenly disintegrated in a hail of bullets. "Look what you made me do," he pouted.

Thurgose clicked off the machine with his nose. "We must begin."

Anton sighed. He was tired of lessons. He could recite enough mathematical theorems to baffle a real mathematician and understood the secrets of science, philosophy and any other subject Thurgose threw at him. He impishly turned the game back on. "It can wait," he decided.

Thurgose moved to the corner controls and slid into place. In an instant, power to the machine stopped. Anton grimaced as his screen went dead. Whoever designed the ship had made sure the horse ruled. Still, he was an adult, and it was time he made a few decisions. He turned and faced the animal. "I am the Frighem, and I tell you what to do," he said sharply. "And I am telling you to turn on my game."

The horse simply slid into the wide screen control panel. "I am programmed to supersede your directions in those instances of extreme importance." While Anton glared petulantly, the little animal opened the front portals. In the right corner of the dark sky, a large object bobbed in space. Anton didn't see it immediately. He was trying to formulate some way to get around Thurgose.

"Look, Brubiscon," Thurgose said. "Your new home."

Anton sat up and slowly put down the game controls. For a moment, he didn't know how to respond. He couldn't believe they had finally arrived at their mysterious destination. He edged closer to the open view and stared into the blackness. The small orb in the corner was rapidly growing in size. It looked greenish-gray now, taking both shape and color quickly.

"How long before we land?" Anton asked.

"When you are ready."

"No sign of Wyron?"

Thurgose flashed a fuchsia color. That meant no. Anton was relieved. Wyron may be chasing, but he had not caught up.

Anton started to turn. "My uniform?"

"No," Thurgose stopped him. "You do not know the language well enough. You do not know the customs. You must be completely prepared for what lays ahead. You must be able to mingle with the people, to learn their mores, to become one of them. You must be, as I must be, able to survive.

"You?"

Thurgose nodded. "Even I, Brubiscon. Even I."

In silence, they stood together and looked at the planet slowly taking shape in front of them. Any fear Anton felt melted away. Instead there was a surge of energy. Glancing over at Thurgose, he began to smile. "We did it," he yelled and began racing around the room. He catapulted across the couch and rolled along the carpet. In an instant, he was back on his feet, yelling loudly. "We did it. We did it."

"Brubiscon," Thurgose cried, "please. We have many more things to do." It moved easily aside as Anton hurled a pillow at him. "There are concerns that must be discussed. There are lessons."

Panted and grinning Anton tossed another pillow at Thurgose and missed. It plopped harmlessly against the wall. "When do we land? What do you know about these people? Come on, tell me," Anton pleaded.

"I have not been programmed to answer your questions," Thurgose said.

Anton petulantly flung the last pillow. "Thurgose!" he protested. "You have to know or you wouldn't have come here." He raised his right hand. "Logic must precede the disorder of spoken thought," he recited. "Thoraster. About 2,000 years ago. Something like that."

"Good," Thurgose said, "but the year is wrong. It was 1145."

"Close enough." Anton began to pace with a mischievous look on his face. "This ship could have been programmed to come this far, but I doubt it. We didn't know of any inhabited planets. Right? Right. I was just sent in hopes of finding one. Therefore, *unitum la folenza*," he said, quoting an old Dalia dictum, "you had to select this site." Thurgose was silent. "You have to be monitoring the planet. How else can you teach me its customs, its language?" He wagged a finger at the horse. "Don't play games now. You've taught me too well."

"We have lessons," Thurgose said.

"We have lessons. We have lessons," Anton mimicked. "I want to know when we land. When do I begin to become part of that?" He pointed defiantly at the planet.

"When you have successfully assimilated your lessons," Thurgose said.

"How about a look first?"

"We are not close enough for sufficient focus."

Anton sighed. The little horse was going to get its way after all. He stared into space at the planet. It seemed a swirl with clouds. Blue coloring was clearly visible. Anton liked that. It reminded him of home. So did the clouds. There seemed to be a single satellite around the planet, not the three he was used to, but it could be Dalia. And there, off in the distance, might be Kajia. It just could be. Perhaps the land had recovered enough. Perhaps the ship had made a giant arc. He moved closer to the window. No. It couldn't be.

There was a sudden sadness. He might never see Dalia again. Maybe there was nothing to go home to. Or maybe there were beings here who would help him return home. Perhaps he could find a mate, build a larger ship, and travel back through space to the azure-crested mountains, the encrusted, treacherous plains. Or perhaps, here he would stay, one among many until his years had ended, until the real measure of time mattered.

He swallowed hard. There was much to do. He would have to dress properly. He would not make an entrance in the clothes of a boy. He would wear his full uniform, no matter what Thurgose said. He would use the weapons of his people to defend himself, and he would survive.

"It is time," Anton said softly. The one-time crown prince of Dalia, the chief flower among the eastern skies, god of youth and firmament, the first son of the great Frighem Laren, son of the great queen Rena, Brubiscon of the Gorean Festival and bearer of the whiten bushels at the festival of Alain ran rose to his full height, about 5 feet, and threw back his shoulders. He took a deep breath and led the way to the learning section by the wall.

Thurgose followed. It slid its wheels into the attachment groves. They made a loud click that seemed to drown out the endless surge of the engines. Behind them, the window closed. Slowly, the small ship began to orbit the planet.

And just as slowly, Thurgose began to teach. "You have heard the language before and seen many broadcasts," it said.

Anton sat up. "This is the source?" he said wide-eyed. He stared at the planet. In history class long ago, he had been told how various programs suddenly began streaming across space. The novelty drew wide attention as scholars slowly deciphered the strange, rhythmic language. Even small schoolchildren became aware of the distant people and their odd behavior. Many learned the language, which served as a runic code for intimate conversations.

Anton was almost conversant in it.

"You will need to learn it better." The horse told Anton. "It is called English."

III

Impatiently, Walter Canyon checked his monitor. The red light wasn't on yet. He leaned back in his chair with a daily news report in his hand. He wasn't actually reading, but the computer didn't know that. The computer couldn't know everything. His right hand aimlessly tapped the desk with a pencil, but he didn't hear the sound. His mind was furiously considering the options: he could have remained the same, or he could have been promoted. Perhaps one level? A few points? He shivered nervously, but hid that, too. Nothing could disturb his outward calm. Perhaps the computer considered demeanor. That could be important, along with appearance.

Canyon was very careful with his outward look. His suit was always neat with each crease in proper alignment. His hair, just beginning to pick up a hint of gray, was carefully brushed and clipped. Not a single strand was out of place. Canyon took the precaution of having his barber trim nose hair, too, edge his eyelashes and eyebrows, and remove any stray hairs from around his ears. If the computer gave points for such things, he had cornered the market. His shoes were polished; his teeth shining. Walter Canyon was a walking advertisement for the modern man on his way up the ratings ladder. Good grooming was expensive, Canyon realized, but his image must be maintained.

His meticulous efforts had helped for the past nine years. Then, abruptly, something had gone dreadfully wrong.

He remembered seeing that month's rating, and being both hurt and surprised to find there had been no change from the previous number. He must have read the number highlighted on his screen five times: 675.45. Lack of progress, even a tenth of a decimal, represented a disaster for an ambitious bureaucrat.

Previously, forward movement up the rating's ladder had always been slow, but steady. The numbers invariably climbed a little higher each month, and, as far as Canyon as concerned, deservedly so, too.

Wasn't he now civilian director for the Army's southwest command? He gazed around his office triumphantly. Lush wood paneled walls, an authentic Krasnayanski painting on the back wall, a leather couch, console controls that activated television and closed circuit viewing. He had come a long way for this.

If only he hadn't come up with a plan to recruit new personnel for the military. How could he have guessed it would go so wrong? Still, he couldn't imagine the computer wouldn't give more consideration to that mishap than to all the good things he accomplished, whatever they were.

Even though the end result wasn't good, Canyon was sure his original idea was ideal: use toothpicks with special promotions, bonuses, assignments or other special prizes attached as an incentive for recruits. The recruits would dig around in the dirt, find a toothpick and delight in finding out what each had won. What could possibly go wrong?

Canyon's assistant, Sinone, had spread the toothpicks across his living room and was carefully connecting the paper prize slips when he had heard the videophone ring. He had stood up and accidently walked barefoot across the toothpicks. As a result, he was in the hospital for two days while surgeons removed the wood from his feet.

Canyon had heard the news with disguised anger. Certainly, he would never let the computer see the outrage, but he suspected Sinone had intentionally hurt himself to detract from Canyon's rating. Why else had he been barefoot? And doing the work at home? That could only be a way of increasing his own standing. Now, Sinone was coming back to work a day early. Again, the computer would see that dedication. Canyon almost spit. Who needed assistants like that? His face whitened as he fought his disgust. The computer must never see that emotion. Lord knew how it would translate such lack of complete self-control.

He glanced toward the side wall. A black eye stared at him. He smiled and suppressed an urge to wave. That damn computer. He was tempted to cover that opening, but that would guarantee his chances for the life drugs became nil. That was the choice all humans made by age 25: Allow the computer complete surveillance power and possibly qualify for drugs that could prolong life for hundreds of years, or shun the observation and live as long as nature intended.

Canyon had opted into the system with delight, convinced of his own abilities. Even now, he was not disappointed. Hadn't McCaulley zoomed to a 3 rating? If a fat non-com like him could do it, then a wiry, tough promotions director certainly could, too.

The computer monitor light blinked.

Recognizing the signal, Canyon calmly put down the report and stood. He smoothed his coat, ran a hand along his hair and tucked in his shirt. In measured steps, he walked around the desk. His shoes created a harsh sound on the tile floor. He liked that. It was almost as though he was being announced. He walked by driving his heels into the floor to emphasize the contact. People knew he was coming long before he arrived.

He set his face: a firm look, a steady gaze: no emotion. He realized his subordinates on the 16th floor would wait for him to read his current status. They would see how calm and assured he was. They would watch him turn and walk back after getting his monthly rating, and they would wonder at his lack of reaction, admire him for the stoical way he received the news. A few inevitably tried to emulate his hardened approach, but with so much dependent on the single readout, few could manage to pull it off. They lacked his will power, Canyon told himself.

The rating room was located on the other side of the building. Canyon had to walk past the secretaries, his assistant's small office, the advertising director's office and the cafeteria to get to it. He enjoyed that brief march. He could feel eyes watching him. He held his head erect, his shoulders back, like a soldier on maneuvers, and strode down the hallway with his shoes pounding out a drum's cadence. Around him, activity ceased.

A director, he was the only one informed when the new ratings were available. Everyone else had to wait until he finished reading his. He knew once he returned to his office, a few brave employees would venture out, and then they would all crowd around the viewer. Everything was coded so no one knew which number referred to a friend, a competitor or a stranger.

They would discuss the results in low whispers, commiserating or congratulating. Most expected to show little gain, but optimism always flared. After all, at least two people in this territory in the last year had been accorded major ratings' jumps although they served in menial capacities. The computer did not explain the changes; it never did.

When Canyon heard about the promotions, he had almost considered resigning and hibernating in a meaningless position. The public relations directorship was open, for example. He fought off that consideration. Few people ever achieved anything from such office. He knew the statistics; he knew the odds. It was a director-ship, but the lowest one on the rating ladder and barely above the custodial staff. He stayed where he was.

Canyon neared the rating room, which did not have a door. As usual, it was well lit, inviting, a cheerful appearance that masked a reality. He marched in.

On the back wall was a large white screen. In front was a computer console. Canyon stepped in front of the console and touched the screen. It recognized his fingerprint and immediately lit up. In turn, the room lights dimmed. In a moment, there was a slight hum. The screen flashed information about date, location and other logistics. There was also a warning about attaining information improperly. Canyon, like everyone else, didn't read it. Mostly, he focused on the screen as anxiety slowly began to boost his pulse.

Without any pause, a series of special codes flashed onto the screen. Only four individuals in the building knew the proper combination. Canyon pressed the appropriate sequence. To his annoyance, his hand was trembling. He could sense the strain in his lower back. And he felt a twinge in his left shoulder. Nerves there always tightened at times like this. He wanted to bite his lips, but would not give the ever-vigilant computer the satisfaction.

He pressed the start button, and a long line of numbers began to roll. His code came and went quickly, but he did not stop the procession, nor try to read it. The computer ran through all 2500 employee names and started over. Only then did Canyon halt the flow.

He scanned down the screen until he came to his number. "Walter Marson Canyon," the encryption told him. He knew the symbols so well. He read the next line. "Previous month: 675.45." His eyes moved across the screen. "This month: 645.89." There was a flashing sign next to it: "B." Canyon knew full well what that letter meant: "individual has decreased standing."

Canyon almost staggered. Last month was bad enough with no change. Now, his rating was falling. He took a deep breath; his legs shook. He felt light-headed, stunned. All he could see was the inevitable decline until, old and gray, he retired to await the final days of life.

Canyon winced as he read the rating again. He forced himself to stand there and think. His rating was falling, and he didn't know why. Could it be Sinone? Canyon had visited him in the hospital. He had demonstrated caring, sympathy, concern. He had even stopped by Sinone's apartment and discarded the toothpicks. He changed the game. Instead, recruits dug around in dirt for pennies. Each penny had a special color and number attached. It had been great fun and very successful.

Canyon's mind raced through other possibilities. The skydiver stunt where the parachutist landed on the Albuquerque highway and was nearly killed? No, Canyon told himself, he had authorized payment. He had been friendly, generous. He had been everything a director should be. Silently, he cursed the computer. This had to change. He suddenly remembered Thomas Veronic. He had jumped out a top-story window suddenly after one rating month. And Luella Hanson: she had shot her boss before committing suicide. He had not understood their behavior then. It was all making sense now. What was he going to do?

Canyon realized he had been in the room for a long time. Others would gossip. They might even guess that his ratings had fallen. He could not be seen to be in a vulnerable position. He smoothed his coat again and adjusted his belt. He turned the lights back up and deactivated the screen.

He felt uncomfortable thoughts cascade about his mind.

Was Sinone getting a promotion? Did someone have to end up in a hospital to receive some consideration? Maybe he could accidently hurt himself? Maybe the computer wanted to test his ability to withstand pain?

Canyon walked into the bright hallway. Heads disappeared from doorways. Chatter stopped instantly. Even the tap-tap-tap of terminals grew silent as he walked by. There were just the harsh, heavy sounds of his shoes as he marched into the office. He kept his eyes on the distant wall, his lips firm and set. Only his eyes showed any ache, and he couldn't figure out how to disguise that, at least not yet.

Sinone met him by the office door. He did not speak but followed Canyon inside the office. He sat in a visitor's chair, uninvited, but calmly. Canyon sat down, folded his hands in front of him and coughed. Business must continue.

"I assume you've completed your report," he said. The words were so loud. They crackled inside his head and broke the silence that had surrounded him since he first saw the light blink.

Sinone smiled. "Which one?" Canyon did not reply for a moment. Why hadn't he been given a dumb assistant, one who didn't turn him into the straight man? Sinone was setting him up. The computer would see the thin, dark man with the placid face was working hard, preparing reports, showing initiative while his boss, who was gradually turning pale, was merely enjoying the fruits of that labor.

"You know which one," Canyon finally said through clenched lips. He forced a smile.

Sinone opened a small briefcase. "Do you mean my report on General McCaulley's visit?"

"That didn't take long, did it?" Canyon asked. He didn't hide his sarcasm.

"I worked on it every night this week," Sinone replied easily. He bent over, revealing his bald spot. His scalp glistened in the soft lights. "As you know, a visit by General McCaulley is extremely important."

Canyon waited impatiently while Sinone flipped through his computer tablet to retrieve the material. McCaulley's visit could mean a break. He was the only military man to achieve a number 3 rating. He got that during his time on the moon 60 years ago, a decade after the computerized rating system started.

The general, then just a corporal, had been stationed on the moon as a sentry, guarding and monitoring basic scientific material. In the only known contact with aliens, he had faced them alone, fighting them off and forcing them to flee. Dazed and bleeding, he had been able to maintain his position, and survive with damaged oxygen and food supplies until help arrived almost four days later.

The effect on the world was astounding, and he was promoted instantly from a middling one to a heroic three rating virtually overnight. Hailed as the type of individual who deserved long life, McCaulley had become the symbol of young men and women eager for near immortality. He had been unknown, a meager pawn in the military machine, yet had managed to rise to glory.

His story brought people like Canyon into the Army, certain they could follow in McCaulley's giant footsteps. Still, scientists and scholars had won the majority of promotions to the second level, where drugs were doled out enough to ensure life for an extra 200 to 300 years. If they proved their value to mankind, they could earn the final promotion to 3. That's all Canyon wanted. If he could just get that second rating, the third would follow. He was sure of that. Getting acquainted with the general couldn't hurt.

As part of his annual inspection, he was coming to Phoenix, to this office. Sinone had drafted a plan; both had already gone over it carefully. Now, Canyon planned to review it again and added any thoughts. After all, it would carry his name as author.

Sinone handed the tablet across the desk. "You heard about Seavers," he said casually.

Distracted from his reading, Canyon sputtered. "No."

"It came across the monitor this morning. I thought perhaps you had read it."

Canyon glared over the tablet. "I was seeing the doctor about my shoulder this morning. Perhaps you remember? I told you yesterday." He watched Sinone wince. A good shot. It was not a good idea to insult a superior. The computer would recognize Sinone's comment for what it was. "What about Colonel Seavers?" He emphasized Seavers' title for show, too. After all, Col. Rutherford Seavers was their boss, chief of the entire western region.

"Perhaps you should call it up," Sinone suggested.

Canyon considered for a moment. If he listened, the computer might record he was willing to heed subordinates. If he didn't pause to check the facts, the computer might note he was a leader and not dependent upon the whims of his assistants. Such conflicting ideas constantly paralyzed his thinking. He pursed his lips and pretended to read what was now the third version. Sinone had made changes on the first page. Who knows what else he had done? And McCaulley was coming in two days.

"All right," Canyon finally agreed and signed onto his terminal.

A message blinked in his private file. He called it up.

The face of Col. Rutherford Seavers appeared before him. It was wan, drawn. "My fellow colleagues," he began, "I have recently received the results of my evaluation." His hands shook on the edge of the screen. Canyon listened carefully. His first 10-year evaluation was coming up, too. It was a dreaded moment with whispered talk of dark rooms, strange questions and a psychological terror that destroyed weak participants. Seavers, a holdover from the past, was obviously still flustered. "I have also been informed I will be transferred effective immediately to a more suitable position, writing programs for NASCAR races."

Canyon heard the death knell in Seavers' voice. His boss had lost the competition. He was being sent to the most meaningless job on the planet, to work there until he retired. It was a death sentence with no immediate execution. He liked Seavers and almost pitied him, but there was a ray of hope in that depression. Seavers' demise meant there was an opening available, a chance to move up. Maybe this was the opportunity he needed. He turned off the monitor.

"We should prepare a party to honor Colonel Seavers," he told Sinone, "and let him know how much we will miss him. I'm sure the promotion is worthy of his talents."

"No doubt," Sinone replied with a sly smile. "I'll think of something."

"Good. Let's get back to our plan for the general's visit," Canyon said, pointing at the report, "where are you going to get the turkeys?"

~ * ~

Sinone suppressed the comment that the whole plan was a turkey, now that Canyon had revised it so completely. Fortunately, he was by nature taciturn. On the other hand, he could see the twitches in his boss' cheek. Given a chance, with the computer not evaluating every moment, Canyon might be tempted to yell, to throw things, to harass anyone and everyone. He had to restrain himself. Sinone loved to prick him, to drive him a step closer to an explosion. Someday, it might happen. Maybe just before the 10-year evaluation. That would be a good time. Then this office would be his.

Sinone craned his neck a bit. The chair would have to go. Canyon opted for the plush, thick-cushioned variety. Not his assistant. Sinone wanted one hard and firm, the kind that characterized a man driven to greatness.

"I still feel the turkeys might be too hard to handle," he finally said.

"You do?" Canyon sneered. "As we discussed, General McCaulley is from Massachusetts, and you know we are near Thanksgiving. What could be more appropriate than turkeys?"

"Pilgrims?"

"And just what would they signify? What kind of message would men in black outfits carrying muskets send? We have plenty of weapons and soldiers here already. Turkeys," Canyon said eagerly, "that's the key."

"Turkeys," Sinone agreed somberly.

"Good, now have you contacted the supplier?"

Sinone nodded. There had been a few heads turning in purchasing, but no one interfered. They were all quite willing to let Canyon hang himself. Who knows? There could just be another empty chair in two days. And if the stunt succeeded, he could get promoted. That, too, would create a vacancy. Anyone on the way up had to consider all the angles.

There were now 40 turkeys en-route from someplace in the Midwest. Sinone hoped they could be diverted into dinners. However, now, each would have a little bib around its scrawny neck welcoming Gen. McCaulley, and every bib would bear Canyon's proud signature. In such ways was greatness achieved.

"I have also arranged the fireworks and the parade," Sinone reported.

"And lined up all the local men originally from the Northeast?"

Another Canyon special. Sinone had spent a week, some of it while still recuperating, arranging with personnel for all soldiers based in the region who were born in the Northeast to be brought to headquarters. There were officers in five states ready to kill him, but the matter had been done. If nothing else, the computer had proof of his logistical ability on its processor. He would know if it did any good next month.

This month's rating would also include the toothpick accident. Thoughtful of him to think of it and so clever of Canyon to give him a chance. Sinone always knew he had a high tolerance of pain. Canyon just gave him the opportunity to prove it. He wondered if Canyon knew the whole thing was arranged. No doubt the director was suspicious. Sinone studied his boss: Lean and stubborn. His eyes sunk deep into his head. Shoulders bent. And the graying hair. Canyon looked so much older than his real age.

Sinone hid a smile. Canyon may be a victim of genetics, or, perhaps, the pressure. A 3 had to withstand a lot of pressure. The computer would note how much this job had aged him.

"Are you feeling better?" Sinone asked.

"What? I'm fine."

"The shoulder, sir. The shoulder."

"It's fine. Tennis. I was playing too much. It's hard to stay in shape with the hours we keep."

Sinone nodded. All for show. It was like a well-rehearsed play. Everything was just for the critical eye of one reviewer, the thin, long lens of the computer. No applause, no curtain. The cast was well rehearsed, however. "Are you satisfied with the plan now, sir?"

"Just a few things," Canyon said. He paused and forced out,

"You did a good job."

~ * ~

He tried to put some actual sentiment into his comment. Always reward subordinates. Good management technique. After all, they were supposed to be a team: Sinone and that new woman who was due to start.

Canyon had been bucking for a second assistant for months. Any important director had a long string of assistants following behind, like a duck with her young. He would direct and orchestrate them until he moved on and up. The woman would be here just in time for the major show for McCaulley. That project was his final proof of the need for more staff.

He re-read the plan again before sending Sinone off to start implementing it. After his aide left, Canyon leaned back to savor the moment. He would never leave the general's side. By the time that day was over, McCaulley would know his name well. The computer would have to be impressed by his new status as a friend of a 3.

There were so many details to arrange. The new assistant, Bonnie Cataline, arrived in time to be thrown headfirst into the middle of arranging masses of moving bands, marching men and curious citizens. There was not a minute for training, but somehow she managed to survive. The two days lengthened beyond sunset, but everything was done in time for McCaulley's visit.

The finally sun rose that morning and Canyon with it. He was relieved the weather report had been promising. No chance of rain or one of the windstorms that blew desert sand across the city.

McCaulley was due to arrive at 9 a.m., 0900 hours military time, and Canyon was on site long before that. He inspected the parade route, resisting the urge to wave at the imaginary crowds. Then he hurried back to be sure the turkeys were in place, chalk was drawn so the bands knew where to begin. The soldiers arrived briskly at 8:30. An honor guard waited at the airport. The rest lined the route into Phoenix.

The military headquarters lay on the outskirts of the sprawling Arizona capital, and there were just enough men to go around. The crowd had already gathered along the route. Sinone distributed flags to those who wanted them, mingling American with those of the Massachusetts Commonwealth and the Army. Finally, at 5 minutes to 9, as the roar of the jet subsided, Canyon took his place at the base of the mobile doorway. It was swung to the private plane's cabin. The door opened and out stepped Gen. Allistair McCaulley, the first seven star general in United States history.

He saluted the officer who greeted him as his escort and began to descend the steps. Somehow, the sun seemed brighter. The row of stars on McCaulley's shoulders gleamed. Standing at the base of the portable stairs, Canyon waited. Photographers busily captured the moment as Canyon, dressed in his classiest Navy blue suit, stepped forward.

The general was even heftier than his pictures implied. Although he seemed young facially, he moved like an old, stiff man, moving first one leg carefully, then the other. He was breathing heavily when he reached the bottom. Canyon moved quickly to salute and then shake hands. The grip was firm, but the hand small.

Canyon was a bit taken aback to see how short the general really was, almost a walking top with a hefty bulge in the middle. He resembled an animated mannequin with starchy skin and a fixed smile. His eyes were warm, at least, a little blue with a persistent sparkle. Canyon guided him to the receiving line where he met the Southwest military leaders, all of them decked out in ribbon-adorned uniform. Canyon and the general then entered the open-topped limousine for the eight-mile ride to the office.

"Damn inspections," McCaulley grumbled. He stood on a box so his head poked through the car's roof window while his ample posterior greeted Canyon. Canyon preferred to peek through the curtained windows to see the flag-waving throng and imagine himself on the receiving end of the cheers.

After a few moments, McCaulley lowered himself with an oomph and plopped on the soft bench across from Canyon. The general was breathing hard from the exertion.

"Being a 3 is a real pain," he confided. "I'm going to have to be on a diet for the next six hundred years. And all I do is go to banquets and eat. How the hell can I lose weight that way?"

Canyon coughed. "Excuse me, sir. Could you draw your attention to the soldiers? They are all from the Northeast. We thought you'd appreciate having some of your neighbors on hand."

"Damn nice thought," McCaulley said after a pause. "Good thinking."

Canyon sighed internally. This was going smoothly.

McCaulley occasionally mounted the box and waved as the limo drove slowly through the throng. En route, McCaulley noted the various state flags. On his next descent, he jabbed Canyon in the ribs. "Your idea?"

"Yes, sir."

"Why can't people in D.C. think like this?"

"Maybe," Canyon said faintly, "the wrong kind of people are in D.C."

McCaulley laughed. "Would you say that louder for the microphone?" He jabbed Canyon again. "Just kidding." He looked around. "No camera. No one has to keep an eye on us three's. I kind of miss the damn thing."

"Yes, sir."

"Bet you don't," McCaulley whooped. "Don't answer. If you say the wrong thing, you'll get a demerit."

The entourage slowly wound its way to the office building. It loomed ahead like a silver knife. Canyon kept up a steady conversation, trying to add a few comments every time there was a lull in the crowd noise. It wasn't easy. There were thousands of people craning for a look. There were not many 3's, and they rarely visited anywhere. McCaulley was the busiest of them all, and this was his first visit to Phoenix. The last 3, a scientist with a bent toward chemistry and young women, had come five years ago unannounced and then left just as quietly after conducting some public research and several hushed-up late night intimate experiments.

By the time the limo stopped in front of the Southwest Army headquarters, McCaulley was breathing hard just from stepping up and down from the box.

The driver opened the limo door in front of the reviewing stand. The soldiers, who had regrouped once the car passed and were marching behind, split into separate formations and swung around the car to take up positions on either side. Both marching bands began to move forward and assume their positions.

Politely, Canyon gestured toward the raised platform jutting into the air above 10 feet above them. He looked at the staircase and then at Canyon. "Can't we stay here?" he asked plaintively. Canyon made a noncommittal shrug. He would have liked to say no. After all, other dignitaries, like General Alsop, were waiting there. McCaulley understood. With a sigh, he followed Canyon from the limo, emerging to a loud cheer.

With Canyon beside him, the band playing and the sun glowing enthusiastically, the general marched to the staircase. He took two steps and almost fell backwards into Canyon. The director groaned, but held him. The impetus started McCaulley going again. In time, they stood side by side behind the microphone.

Canyon held up his hands for silence. There was a hush. This was the moment. Let the computer record all this, Canyon insisted silently. Let it see a great leader in action.

"General McCaulley," he said. His voice roared through the crowd. "It is with great pleasure we welcome you to Phoenix." The crowd screamed. Canyon waved for quiet. "Knowing how far you are from your home state, we thought we'd begin with a little memento." He pointed to the side where Sinone stood. All eyes followed. Grandly, Sinone nodded, he bowed and smiled at the crowd.

"General," Canyon intoned, "I give you a few of your native residents." Sinone opened the small door leading to the turkey pen. One or two of the birds poked their heads out. The crowd laughed. A few more wandered out. McCaulley smiled. Canyon took a deep breath. The general was going to say how pleased he was by the idea. Newspaper cameras were rolling; photographers were snapping away. He was going to announce that such ideas deserved special consideration, that there was room for such bright men in Washington. That a promotion was the only just reward. That there was even room on his staff for such an innovator. The general was going to say all that. Canyon could see it in his blue eyes, in his smile. But the words never reached his mouth. They never had a chance.

Suddenly, the air was alive with turkeys. They hurtled out of their little pen and launched themselves into the crowd. Feathers were everywhere. Band members fought them talon and claw to drumsticks and trombones. One enterprising turkey dove into a tuba and stuck there. Others assaulted the soldiers. Chaos reigned. Sinone tried shooing the birds back into the pen, but they were not the least obliging. They waddled off. A few careened into the speaker's dais.

"Fascinating," McCaulley said. "Good thing I'm not from Arkansas. They like wild pigs, you know."

Canyon paled rapidly. Turkeys fly? No one told him that. He had visions of these big birds kind of leading the parade past the general, pecking at the ground and making a little noise. These birds were doing anything but. One had landed on the open roof of the limousine and quickly taken up residence inside. Others were flailing away at spectators. Canyon saw photographers capturing every moment, the TV cameras turning, and felt his legs sag. His name was on every bib.

He leaned against the microphone. "Oh," he managed. Everything was going away: his promotion, his dreams. And it was all his fault. How could he do this to himself? He took a deep breath. Let the computer know he could handle himself in an emergency.

"Ladies and gentlemen," he began.

McCaulley tapped his arm. "Perhaps you'd better address the birds. They seem to be causing all of the ruckus."

Canyon fought against panic rising inside. He turned to reply to McCaulley, but stopped. The general had put a turkey feather in his hat. It stuck up straight in the back. Other feathers were drifting like snow across his uniform. Canyon looked down at himself. He, too, was a mass of white feathers. His carefully orchestrated appearance had disappeared. He tried to swallow, and there was a feather in his mouth. He just closed his eyes. "General," he said, "I'm so sorry."

"No need to," McCaulley assured him. "But, I must say, you have interesting ideas." He surveyed the disarray with a hungry look. "Tell me, were those supposed to be our lunches?" Canyon just shook his head. McCaulley sighed. "Too bad," he remarked. "I do love fresh turkey." He pointed at a dead bird by the corner and waved to an aide. "Save that one for dinner," he called.

"General," Canyon tried again. Words failed him. Everything failed him.

"By the way," McCaulley said in a half whisper, "I'm from Ohio originally and only live in Massachusetts now. But I like the thought anyway."

Canyon barely heard him. In the background, a couple of members of the disorganized band were playing "Stars and Stripes Forever" and a whole chorus of people were singing "…A duck may be somebody's mother."

"Don't worry," Sinone told him later, after the debris had been cleared and the general had been safely deposited into his hotel for the afternoon, "some poor director somewhere else is going to be hard pressed to top this."

Try as he might, Canyon just couldn't find consolation in that. But he still tried. For the next week, he tried.

IV

With a sweeping gesture, Anton flung open his closet door. There was his formal, regal attire, properly cleaned, ready to be worn. As air struck the wrapping, the plastic melted away, exposing it to view. It seemed so inviting as if just waiting for this moment to arrive.

Anton had looked at it dozens of times in the past few years. He visited his closet whenever he began to doubt himself. Opening the door, he always drank in the splendid view, and he would know he must continue. The time had finally come. Thurgose had invited him to dress.

Almost reverently, he removed the suit and put it on his bed. It was even brighter in the soft bedroom light. For a moment, he admired it in awe. He caressed the soft, colorful material. It would fit him perfectly. He just knew it would. In silence, he stripped off his thin shirt and pants. He put the nuvras to one side. His feet had a nice scar pattern across the arch now. While they were not visible when he wore his shoes, he resolved to find a time to take them off when it would cause the greatest sensation. Thurgose told him to be patient, and he promised to be.

He put his pants on first. The loops meshed exactly at his waist and closed nicely. He felt as though he had been wearing them forever. The rainbow shirt was next. The colors blended and changed tones as the light splayed across it. The golden jacket followed. It slipped easily over his head and molded itself to his thin frame. His nuvras came last. Anton then strutted to the mirror and stood there, admiring himself.

He had seen the outfit used in ceremonies only one time before, when a cousin was installed as coordinator of educational services. Anton could almost see that day again in the mirror. He was standing to one side on a balcony overlooking the scene. His father was next to him. The image was a bit muddy with time. There was a gasp as his cousin entered: tall, strong and encased in the golden coat of manhood. He strode like a monarch down the central aisle. Even from his distant vantage point, Anton had been able to see the pride on the young man's face.

His father had patted his head. "Someday," he said quietly, "that will be you." Anton had looked up into the wise, old face and nodded bravely.

Even now, Anton could still see his cousin's soft black hair glistening in the light. Then, the image faded. That was long ago. Everyone in that room, except him, was dead. Anton ran a comb through his hair and forced a smile. This was how his cousin looked. And this must have been the way he felt before the great terracotta doors opened and he marched into the hall, his nuvras making sharp slapping noises on the hard basalt floors.

With one last look at his reflection, Anton turned and began to march down to the living quarters. His eyes stared straight ahead. He could imagine the hushed whispers, the background orchestra. He sensed the awe and admiration in the thousands of eyes that watched his every move. Never had he been so sure of himself or so proud.

"Brubiscon," Thurgose interrupted, "perhaps you will avail yourself of my problem."

The voice, coming as seemed to from his imaginary, admiring throng, startled Anton, but he recovered quickly. He sighed and glanced over at Thurgose. The little horse was nuzzling a series of knobs by the central control.

"How do I look?" Anton asked, whirling so his companion could see a complete picture.

"You have the proper attire of a person of your stature. However," Thurgose said, "I would suspect a sash would complete the appearance."

Anton blushed and hurried back to his room. Of course, the sash. He found it on the floor where it had slipped. Green, gold and red, it was designed to run from his right shoulder, around the loop at his waist and back up. At one time, it would have been metallic and used in fighting. Now, it was just ornamental cloth.

Again, he glanced in the mirror. No wonder everyone was murmuring, he told himself with a wry smile. Why, the Frighem had been dressed like a lowly butler without his sash of office. How humiliating. It was a good thing only Thurgose was around to see it. If something similar had happened on Dalia...Anton stopped himself. Of course, it wouldn't have happened on Dalia. There would have been ministers of state to verify each article of clothing, to tutor him in the proper phrases and guide his every step. There would have been vectors and assigniaries, all to be sure the sash was the right color, where it belonged, properly tied and perfectly aligned. Without such assistance, mistakes were bound to happen. So he shrugged it all off and went looking for Thurgose. The creature was still at the controls.

"Are you ready to avail yourself now?" it asked.

"Certainly," Anton replied in surprise. How odd. The horse never needed assistance. It was always the other way around.

"Oh," Thurgose moaned most uncharacteristically. "Such a concern." It spun around to look at Anton in obvious frustration. "I am trying to program my memory packs. I do not expect to be in contact with our ship on all occasions. Have you a suggestion as to which memories I should retain?"

Anton almost laughed. The poor thing only had room for a handful of packs. Confronted with dozens of choices, it literally did not know what to do. He relished the picture. It was nice to see Thurgose stuck for an answer. "Logic," the teenager said.

Thurgose nodded. "I have chosen that procedure. Therefore, I have eliminated philosophy and religion. Such topics are of no value. I did feel history was significant. And science. I do not know enough about the individuals we will meet to trust their knowledge levels. I also felt a language program could be of importance. Your writing has never achieved expected levels so I have added one for that. And a self-defense program. One for identification of indigenous flora and fauna. One for directional mobility." There was a helpless sound creeping into Thurgose's mechanical voice. "That required an astronomy tape. We will navigate by the stellar projections. I also determined atmospheric decoders were required as well as medicinal concepts." It spun its wheels without moving. "I realized if I kept this up, I would be too laden to function meaningfully. That could jeopardize your safety. I also only have room for four such discs in my control sector."

"Well," Anton laughed, "no one could think of everything."

"I do not think this is humorous," Thurgose retorted. "I would like to intake your suggestions now."

They settled on four selections: medicine, flora and fauna, language and defense. As they considered each disc in turn, Anton felt a chill come over him. They were really going this time. No more wondering. No more waiting and looking out at the planet they circled. They were going to land and attempt to merge with a people there. For this, Thurgose had no tapes, no pre-programmed plans. Anton was frightened, no matter how much he told himself he wasn't. The excitement came with the anticipation; fear came with the reality.

"I have selected a landing site," Thurgose said. "It is located in an acrid region much like Dalia. That will give us the opportunity to acclimate ourselves before attempting to make contact."

Anton gazed through the window. "Do you think they will detect us?"

"They are not on a superior level of sophistication," Thurgose said. "I have circumscribed metal satellites in the lower atmosphere, but am unaware of any ozone detection units. We have been orbiting at more than twenty-two Earth miles above the surface, beyond the range of their highest satellite. I suspect there are ground devices, but I believe we can circumvent those with proper equipment. I will activate our disorientation beams upon entry. Meanwhile, I am initiating a zetzib to disorient tracking devices. Others I can send erroneous messages to."

"Then we are all set," Anton said. He gazed at the distant orb. "I am ready."

"After you eat and I charge my batteries, we will descend," Thurgose said. "We must not find ourselves without provisions. We will stay close to our ship."

"What are they like?" Anton mused half aloud.

"You are similar in appearance, bipedal with a spine," Thurgose told him. "They are taller and of mixed colors, but their colors do not change as yours do. They have ear flaps. I do not doubt their DNA is incompatible."

"I mean in ideas, values. How would they treat an alien?" Anton asked. Thurgose made no answer. That was something they would have to find out.

Suddenly, Thurgose sped to the central control panel. It stared intently at dials. Then, as quickly, lights were turned off; the shield closed. The little horse rapidly pressed buttons while its rockers constantly changed colors. Anton realized the engines had been muffled. Thurgose even silenced the refrigeration unit in the kitchen.

"What is it?" Anton whispered. Thurgose did not answer, but continually carefully scanned each sector of the ship's exterior. "I believe," it finally said in a hushed tone, "I have finally made contact with another vessel in the vicinity."

Anton swallowed hard. "From the planet?" If the inhabitants had sent up a defense ship, or a scout, then they must have more highly sophisticated detection gear than suspected. He could be targeted before he had a chance to even get started. There would be no time to reconnoiter, no time even to evaluate or prepare. He closed his eyes and waited for Thurgose to provide some clue.

Thurgose jabbed at several buttons. "Be seated," he ordered. Anton obeyed. There was obvious intensity in Thurgose's command. The creature was not emotional. Other robotic styles were programmed to use emotion, but Thurgose was given only a limited capacity. His little body glowed pink as circuits began to flood with power. In seconds, it monitored hundreds of swift flowing messages from the various detectors.

Anton tightened the seat belt around his waist and adjusted the shoulder harness. At times like this, he felt alone, piniamed to the pilot chair, looking at a blank wall that should open onto the universe. He lay back and waited, not sure if he would hear the sound of the engine or the concussion of an exploding rocket. The engine roared first.

"I must accelerate," Thurgose said. "There is no time."

"What's out there?" Anton managed to say before the thrust of the powerful engines blocked the words. He felt himself driven into the soft seat. His hands turned white on the arm rest. Behind him, Thurgose rocked backwards. Its wheels locked firmly in place prevented it from being thrown into the back wall. In less than a minute, pressure equalized as the small ship fled from its orbit.

Thurgose quickly scanned the visual readout running across the screen. "Initial results indicate a high level of hulstone essence. That would likely come from Kajia."

"Wyron," Anton breathed. He did not get up. Thurgose would let him know when it was safe. It could be hours. He tried to think. Would the Kajan prefer to destroy the ship or capture him alive? What would he do? The image hardened. For destroying his planet, killing his family, ruining his life? There was only one option: death, quickly and with as much pain as possible. His mind moved on. Wyron would think the same way, especially if he got his hands on Anton. He could be left adrift in space with a minimum amount of air. That would be dreadful. Anton felt tears well up in his eyes. He shook his head to clear away the idea. He was not going to die.

He steadied himself. If the Kajan drew close, he would be met with advanced weapons. Anton's ship came properly equipped with cutting laser lights on both sides, and a shield front and aft. Anton knew which button to push to activate an offensive barrage. The ship itself would handle the aiming. He would guide the killing lights.

He mapped out the scenario as though playing another video game. He could see the fiery red of Kajia against the gold of Dalia, dueling in the mist of space. Then, enthralled with awe and delight, he would watch as Wyron's ship explodes.

Anton unsnapped his belt. Why not now? Why wait? He was not going to be hunted. He was a Frighem now, not some desert quahog. They begged for a little water and sold themselves for food. He would not degrade himself.

"Do not attempt to disengage yourself," Thurgose said in that maddeningly calm voice. "Do not unhook that shoulder strap." The ship lurched, throwing Anton violently from side to side. He hit the strap hard, and the leather cut into him. For a moment, he didn't feel it. Then his right shoulder began to ache. He rubbed the sore area. Perhaps fighting Wyron could wait until he healed. The engines whined. Again, the pressure equalized.

"Where is he?" Anton asked. His voice was weak, a comical imitation of the great roar he felt inside.

"Less than five hundred interspace miles. I have activated disorientation motion, and I do not think he can sense them. They are of a new design, and his ship is of older vintage. It is a wonder Kajia sent out its prince in such style." Thurgose pressed a button, and the screen to Anton's right came alive.

For the first time, he could see his opposition. The picture was just frozen in space: a red blob moving slowly in a direction parallel to his ship. The image magnified, and he could see the Kajan vessel clearly. From the slight protrusion on the underbelly, he could recognize the ship was at least 40 years old. It had the old landing module, which could not be disengaged, unlike the more modern ones that could be jettisoned in the event of a mishap. Landing was then accomplished by gliding, relying on special friction pads on the fuselage. If Wyron lost his module, he would eventually crash. Anton was sure Thurgose noted that, too. It was interesting. Had the Kajans been so short of time that they could not prepare a modern ship? Were there no modern ships on hand? How was that possible? They started the war. They had to be ready. Anton tried to apply logic.

"Possibilities," he murmured. "If the obvious is not sufficient, review those hidden and obscure possibilities." Were there more ships? Could be other ships had chosen different directions, and this one, an old scout, had merely been headed this way and made contact? Another likelihood. This was not a Kajan vessel, but one that looked like it and came from another culture. Less likely. "Information always increases the number of possibilities," he continued, citing the second Dalian axiom. He raised his voice. "Thurgose, what can you tell me?"

"The other ship has locked onto our position," the creature replied. Anton nodded. Then it must be piloted. "It is not moving to engage, but merely to retain visual contact," Thurgose continued.

Anton considered that. Perhaps it was unarmed. Or, perhaps, it was unsure of the identity of the Dalian ship. A thought rushed into his mind. What if Wyron did not realize someone had escaped from Dalia? What if the Kajan was watching his monitor in amazement, trying to identify, asking himself the same question? Anton relished that idea. Served the groka right. What this called for was a surprise move.

He started to get out of his chair when another thought struck him. Wyron may be waiting for that, setting a trap. Sure, use an old ship, lure the enemy close and then strike with the sleek modern attackers kept in reserve. Anton slumped back. He didn't like where all this logic was leading him. It was supposed to supply answers, not more questions. He rubbed his shoulder and distracted himself. Enough of this.

"I think we will seek appropriate refuge," Thurgose said.

"Are other planets in this solar system habitable?" Anton tried.

"No."

"Then what?"

Thurgose did not reply, but was busy reordering the locational devices. It paused to receive a fresh supply of data and then unlocked itself to roll to the recharger and plug itself in. "Perhaps," it said as the pink slowly faded to be replaced by the normal clear color, "you should consider eating, too?"

"And changing clothes?"

Thurgose nodded. "I fear you will need alternative dress in our new destination."

"New language?"

Thurgose nodded again.

Anton slowly unlocked the restraints. They clicked loudly. He stood up. His coat was wrinkled. He could see a small slash on the shoulder; a drop of dark blood marred its golden appearance. He rose unsteadily and felt the hum of the engine once more through the floor. It jangled against his legs and rose through him. Unsteadily, he walked toward the back. His nuvras slapped hard against the steel, echoing loudly inside the cabin. In a minute or two, he was back in the bedroom. His clothes lay on the bed. They were clean. Thurgose had managed everything. It knew better than to discard them. Anton would figure a way to repair the coat. Maybe he wasn't supposed to wear it.

He took off the pants and hung them up first. Plastic formed around them. He then hung the coat up. In the quiet, he dressed slowly. Then he kicked off the nuvras and put them in the closet, too. When he was a man, there would be time to wear them. For now, he was a child, guided by a horse, limited to a play world of solid metal. When he was a man and faced the great universe, then he would put on his shoes. He smiled. Then he wouldn't need his shoes or his coat or his sash. Then, people would know his true status without all that.

V

Anton strained to listen to whatever was going on inside the simple adobe hut across from the parked spaceship. He could hear Thurgose talking in some strange language, but he was tired of drawing circles in the dust with his bare feet. He finally stood up and gazed into the night sky. None of this planet's moons were visible, but they were smaller than he was used to and seemed just to run endless, rapid rings across the heavens. Somewhere out there, Wyron waited.

The Kajan's ship was nothing more than another star. But it was coming. Thurgose was sure of it. It had analyzed the data. The Dalian space craft was sleeker, faster and more modern, but Thurgose could not completely disguise engine emanations, particularly if the trailing vessel had its detection unit properly synchronized. They both had watched the Kajan ship wander through the darkness, seeking to pick up the tell-tale traces before they dissipated completely.

As they sped away, Thurgose continued to monitor. In time, the Kajan was left far behind. At one point, Thurgose circled to see if Wyron was still following. He was. Slowly, almost lumbering, the Kajan vessel had honed in on the scent. There was only speed left, and Thurgose spared none. However, that also meant a change in plans.

"We will have to resuscitate the engines," it announced. "I do not believe we can sustain this propulsion level."

The journey was supposed to have ended by now. The ship was not equipped for a longer run, especially not at full speed.

Anton agreed. The small ship shuddered every now and then as the strain affected it. The closest inhabitable site would have to do. Thurgose reluctantly retreated to the brig to scan the nearest planets. Anton watched the horse with sadness. The little creature wanted to plan, to organize properly. This change was ruining everything. His anger increased.

The Kajans were at it again, Anton seethed. It wasn't enough they had ruined his past; now they were starting on his present. He cursed the enemy that slowly tracked him.

Thurgose would not fight unless forced to although its muzzle came equipped with a special gun. The beam could be fired through one or both nostrils. At the same time, it had activated the detonating device. As a last resort, Thurgose could sacrifice itself to save Anton. Anton could see the weapons through the horse's clear plastic skin, but said nothing. The actions themselves were more eloquent than any words.

In a short while, their ship circled the chosen planet twice. It was a maze of rocks and hills. Thurgose had quickly discovered the hills were merely piles of shale and schist. The ship would not survive a landing on them. The flat plains were shifting sand. When the sun reflected off the barren landscape, it created a blinding light that was almost unbearable. The land shimmered. There were few signs of life. Anton was not unhappy about that. Having muddled through the English language mire, he had no desire to set foot on any other such dismal terrain. Thurgose didn't even try to make him.

Finally, the creature had isolated a flat, hard area in the northern region. Much like Dalia, this planet had most of its plant life congregated in this region. Another site, not far away, while clearly well-tended and filled with flora and fauna, seemed too dangerous. Thurgose refused to risk landing in a well-populated area where the natives could overwhelm the ship's meager defenses.

It guided the ship to a safe, relaxed stop on the baked soil. Peering through the portal, Anton had surveyed the landscape. Large trees seemed eerie in the twilight. He saw a figure move into the shadows. Thurgose came at his call and scurried to the front door. Anton waited while Thurgose greeted a short, round and hairy creature. It was a bipedal, but seemed to roll more than walk. It had two arms, two legs and an apparent tail. Later, Anton discovered the tail was merely a pair of suspenders dragged lazily behind.

Nothing about the being looked dangerous except for something he carried in his right hand, which turned out to be a sheaf of official government papers. He greeted Thurgose with a casual wave and tried to talk. Anton could see Thurgose changing colors as it quickly exhausted its language tape repertoire. Eventually, it stood there mute. Anton relished that. The little creature rarely was lost.

Finally, the being gestured toward the adobe hut and had waddled back, oblivious to whether Thurgose followed or not.

The horse returned to the ship to retrieve Anton. It insisted he take a cloak. A cold wind, not visible from the ship, drifted across every now and then. Besides, Thurgose pointed out, microbes here could be dangerous. His meters had not detected anything injurious to Dalian health, but it was trained to take no chances. Anton obeyed. He took supplies in a small bag and followed.

That's how he found himself seated on the bench, watching the heavens and playing in the dust. Once in a while, he could hear what sounded like large cracks in the distance, but the noise came no closer, and he stopped being suspicious. Instead, he simply grew more impatient. He finally nibbled on a small piece of dydala Thurgose had put into the bag. He wasn't hungry, but there were just so many circles anyone could draw, just so many trees one could watch stand almost motionless, and only so many stars one could admire from afar.

Finally, Thurgose appeared. It looked a bit rundown, having had only a chance to gulp a bit of power before hurrying to this discussion. Shifting from one jump drive to another was very draining.

"I believe we had achieved some level of communication," it said. "We are on Quito in what is called the Backwards. Sra Hugensta, our host, is a government agent assigned to this region." There was almost a sigh there. There were always government agents somewhere. "He thought we were tourists. I have been informed the frynck fights do not occur until tomorrow night."

"Just our luck," Anton cried in mock seriousness. He drew himself up. "I'm not going home until we see them. What will our friends say if they think we've come this far and not seen the frynck fights."

"It's pronounced free-ink," Thurgose said. "You are not listening."

"I heard about the fights, didn't I?"

The creature shook its head. "In respect to your wishes and safety, Brubiscon, we will stay. The atmospheric considerations take precedent over sightseeing options. I understand we have located sufficient current to refuel both our engines and myself. I do not know, but I believe you will be able to digest their food. Their digestive systems are very similar to yours. However, I have yet to detect anything palatable. There is still food on board of course."

Anton stood up. "Now what?"

"More forms," Thurgose said.

It rolled back to the hut. Anton followed and peered into the open doorway. Thurgose held a pen in its mouth and was mournfully filling out the first of what appeared to be endless pages. There was total resignation in its manner. Anton vowed silently that no new government he planned to found would have forms. At least, on Dalia, paperwork had been replaced by electronic images. Quito did not seem as advanced.

Perhaps he should consider taking over this country? The agent looked harmless enough. On the other hand, as far as he could tell, there wasn't very much here. That was a problem. There was little to fight over. But this was a tough land. He walked out onto the ground and bent over. The soil was filled with quartz, gypsum and slate. It hurt his fingers as it broke off into sharp edges. This was a good soil for creating scars. For a moment, he wished he had brought his nuvras. He would develop an excellent series of scars in such a land. And it wouldn't take long either.

With night coming on so rapidly, he couldn't be sure of this world's color. There was obviously green. The ground, no doubt, held pinks, blues, and silvers. He listened for birds, but heard none. Just those sharp cracks in the distance. What strange beings were creating them? He edged back to the hut. The light seemed reassuring. As he backed up, he felt a presence. Before he could turn, Thurgose had inserted itself between him and a tall, thin stranger.

The Quitoan said something. Thurgose replied. Anton tried to understand, but the words were impossible. Just a series of grunts, whistles and moans. How was anyone supposed to make sense of that?

Thurgose readied his weapon and pressed against Anton's leg. "It wants some money," the horse reported.

"I am carrying just a few kylacks. They are worthless here," Anton said.

The native looked at him. Anton could see him now in the light. It was a grizzly-faced being with black eyes. Bent and worn, he held one hand around a tattered vest, another at his side.

"Be quiet, Brubiscon," Thurgose said. "He is bearing something metallic. I cannot see it."

The native said something else.

"Don't shoot," Anton hissed at Thurgose. "We do not know their laws."

Thurgose did not reply. The native repeated its request. Anton could hear the question although he could not understand the words. There were elements of similarity in language, and he had studied too many not to pick up something.

Thurgose said something sharply. The native pulled back with wide-eyed shock. It was a fake emotion. Anton saw clearly through it. He wanted to strike the man and send him away. Who was he to challenge a Frighem? But Thurgose's presence held him. He was also shaking. This was the first time he had ever felt a direct threat, and the chill cut through him. He was angry at himself for showing such weakness, but suddenly, his shoulder ached; his head hurt. So he waited.

The man edged his left hand toward his vest. It hung in ribbons to his knees, and covered both a dirty shirt and a portion of his full-length pants. Anton permitted himself a glance at the shoes. The feet were sheathed in some sort of leather. Obviously, this was not a creature worthy of a Dalian man. That realization helped calm Anton. Maybe the natives were all like this.

The man's hand moved toward the vest faster now. He was smiling, showing a straight row of teeth across the mouth. They were dirty. His gums had sagged down. For the first time, Anton felt the man's breath. It reeked of something strong and awful. He held his own. The man seemed to straighten, as if preparing himself for some attack. The body motion was obvious. Thurgose tightened the trigger. There was a faint, but obvious green glow in its scalp. Only a fool didn't know what that meant.

For just a moment, nothing happened: the man's hand remained poised by the vest; Thurgose hesitated with its green skull glowing. Anton breathed softly.

Then, there was movement in the doorway. The agent appeared. He looked out, scratched his rear end and muttered something. Almost as his words reached Anton, the stranger was gone. He ran unsteadily into the dark shadows and was out of sight in seconds. Anton had to look at the footprints to be sure someone had been there. The green in Thurgose's head faded. The agent said something else and turned back.

"He wants me to finish," Thurgose reported. "It seems he is due to exit for the evening and cannot until I complete the written exercises." It started to roll toward the door and then halted. "Come with me," it requested. "I cannot do as directed and concern myself with your protection."

Anton picked up the bag and followed. His pulse did not begin to slow down until a few minutes later.

Mostly, he was angry at himself for being scared. It was not right. He should have stepped around Thurgose and demanded the native leave them alone. That was a delightful picture to conjure up. Hand pointed dramatically, head thrust back, feet dug into the soil. "Be gone," he should have shouted, overawing the native and his petty request. The image faded soon enough as he looked around at the astonishing display inside the hut.

One wall of the hut was an immense computer, complete with viewing screens, readouts, digital analyzers. Although larger than similar ones on Dalia, it clearly could handle all the data a Dalia computer could. Yet it sat on dirt, backed by stone. The side wall, behind a simple wooden desk, featured modern geological, astronomical and seismological equipment. Small arms ran across endless electronic plates, leaving dark lines in their wake. There seemed no end to the equipment. It sat there, efficiently and quietly working. Overhead, there was a bare light bulb. It seemed so out-of-place, Anton almost stared at it.

He finally wandered over to the side wall to look at the devices. They were well-made and easily on par with anything he had trained on. The weather readings were complete: barometer, inversions, temperature, and the like. Anton could not understand the readings, but recognized the principles. Some of the gadgets notated numbers for uncertain elements, to be sure, but, overall, he felt relaxed with it. Given a few days with the language, he felt confident he could master anything these people had available.

Then he looked at the agent. What a strange creature to be entrusted with such delicate instruments. Remains of a recent meal clung to his stubble. His flat, heavy nose had a steady leak. Uncombed hair cascaded across deep ear ridges on both sides. His clothes were clearly unwashed. As Anton watched, the agent turned and spat. The spittle clung to the computer. It obviously had often been a target, based on the dried markings everywhere.

The agent pulled something out of his front shirt pocket and stuck it in his mouth. It looked like a thin, black, twisted cigarette. He lit it by striking a match on the table. Blue smoke engulfed his face. Coughing and waving his arms, Anton backed away. It was the same noxious odor that contaminated the panhandler's breath. It clung to Anton, almost leaping across the room to reach him. The agent grinned through the haze and held out a cigarette. Anton shook his head.

Thurgose looked up. A pink light glowed in its forehead as it ran an analysis.

"Don't avail yourself." it said, not pausing in its writing, but talking around the pen. "It has a slight amphetamine quality."

"Not to mention an odor," Anton coughed. Good thing he hadn't worn his gold suit. It would have had to be fumigated. As it was, these clothes were going to be tossed at the first opportunity. And nothing Thurgose could say would save them. The creature had a fondness of preserving anything—almost as if its protective urge toward Anton was also directed at everything Anton came into contact with. Not this time, Anton vowed. And if Thurgose didn't finish soon, it was going to witness the rapid departure of one thoroughly overwhelmed, teary-eyed Frighem.

He backed to the doorway, turning now and then to catch his breath. Outside, the sharp cracks were getting louder and closer. Thurgose did not respond to them, but continued scrawling. The agent did not move, but leaned up against the computer, contently smoking. Once in a while, he knocked ashes into a small container inside the computer. Anton gagged at that. What sort of machine was that? Maybe it was addicted to the stuff too. What else? After being forced to stay in this small hovel with that agent, it probably was addicted to something narcotic.

"Done," Thurgose said. It dropped the pen wearily. The agent took the papers and slid them into the computer. It was as though he dropped it into a wastebasket, but the great machine sputtered and came to life. Lights burst on across a front panel. It burped once or twice; then a long pool of dark brown tape appeared at the other. The agent retrieved it, dangling it carelessly over his brawny arms. He snipped off an end with his teeth and handed it to Thurgose. He then held out a second strip of paper toward Anton. The horse took it for him.

It analyzed the tape quickly and then passed it along. Anton took it from Thurgose's mouth. The tape was soft and pliable. Almost reluctantly, he stuck it to his shirt, and it stayed. He didn't quite understand that—there hadn't been any obvious glue—but there it was. He could look down and see it defying him.

"It's our passport," Thurgose told him. "Do not lose it or we will be forced to abide in this facility far longer than either of us intend." With that, the horse rolled to the door. "We must reside this night in the nearest city. We will find sufficient energy resources there to enable us to continue our journey." It rolled out into the night.

Anton stopped by the old bench. He could see the stars above. Somewhere, Wyron waited. He heard the agent walk away, his heavy boots thudding hard against the soil. There were more cracks to the right. Anton looked that way. He could see a faint aura of light through the grove of trees. There was a small, beaten path leading in that direction. It looks like an invitation, he decided. Thurgose was waiting on the edge of the woods, but obviously planning to go in another direction. Anton smiled to himself. It would be nice to shake the little creature up. What good was visiting a planet if they didn't see the sights? Besides, it was early. He felt eager to explore. So he did.

Thurgose almost beat him into the woods, but not quite. It stared up at Anton. "Brubiscon, what is on your mind?" it demanded.

He shrugged. "A stroll." The cracks were loud and constant; the light brighter.

Thurgose turned slightly pink at the noise. "Fools rush to strange sounds," it quoted solemnly.

"Hey," Anton protested. "I'm the one who's supposed to learn philosophy."

"I hear the sounds, too," the horse assured him.

"Next time," Anton said firmly, "you teach, but don't listen. Why can't you be like every other teacher I've known?" He turned and walked slowly up the path. Clucking anxiously, Thurgose followed.

The light was getting brighter. Now, Anton could see the trees clearly. They had thick, smooth bark with fronds appearing about six feet above the ground. Around them were smaller such trees. Both the offspring and adults seemed very dangerous with sharp needles clearly visible from the end of their leaves. Anton walked gingerly to avoid contact. He could imagine what would happen.

He also noticed the ground. Around the base of the trees, the dirt was dark and rich. The shadows created by the wide fronds did not disguise the soil, nor could they hide its rich properties. He knelt and picked up a sample. It hung together in a soft ball, not like the dried crystalline-like dirt in the clearing. He sniffed a bit. The noxious odor clung here, too. Clearly this planet needed a good bathing. So would he if he stayed much longer. He quickly dropped the dirt.

It fell on the path. Again, the contrast between dark and light, rich and dry, was so intense. Thurgose moved up quickly to check the dirt.

"High nitrogen content," it announced. "It also has an enormous quantity of nutrients. This tree is very well provisioned."

Anton paused to blink. Logic, he told himself. These trees obviously helped the soil. No wonder the natives endured the aroma. Yet, the agent was smoking a leaf. Perhaps he and Thurgose had wandered into a preserve where the trees were grown for later consumption. There were such things on Dalia.

They walked on. The cracks were now very loud, the lights even brighter. It was as if they were walking toward an earthbound sun. In a moment, they could hear voices. Workers were grunting and talking to each other. There was an occasional laugh. And there was something else. The strong, pungent odor Anton had grown to recognize floated toward them. There were few breezes in the forest. Anton thought one good gust would clear the air out, but none was likely. It didn't look as though even water could penetrate this thick growth.

Suddenly, they were in a clearing. Anton stood and gaped. Great trees lay stretched out. Natives with thick knives were attacking them, hacking them into small pieces. Their knives hitting the tough exteriors were creating the harsh cracks. A circle of quartz lamps surrounded the workers.

Each of the natives—Anton counted seven—wore aprons bespattered with thick green sap. Their gloves were lanced with hundreds of needles. Behind them, just beyond the circle of lights, another native was standing in the back of a large vehicle which was equipped with threads instead of tires. A smaller native was in the process of lifting some sections of trees to the worker inside the vehicle's back. Another native was piling up leaves to one side. They were all sweaty; their clothes as grimy as those worn by the panhandler.

One saw Anton and shouted. They all looked up. Suddenly, the air was very quiet and very still again. One said something. A native on the side held up a small dark weapon and pointed it. The group began to move together to face Anton and Thurgose.

"Say something," Anton hissed.

Thurgose slipped between Anton's legs and moved in front. Again, its head began to glow a light green. It opened the sheath over its nostrils as it spoke. The natives stopped. Thurgose said something else. One of the natives, clearly a leader, held up his hand and replied. Thurgose answered. The leader smiled.

Anton listened. He could not even understand the sense of what was going on. The natives were tense, as though they were caught doing something wrong. Weren't they supposed to chop down these trees? Why? There were so many in all directions. The trees seemed to cover every inch of soil. Yet, he could see the tension. It was as strong as the odor from the butchered plants. The native by the truck began to lift pieces again. The leader and another worker talked. No one chopped, but pieces already on the ground and the leaves were moved quickly to the truck.

"What's happening?" Anton whispered.

"They're deciding if they should kill us or not," Thurgose replied. It said that very calmly. The leader paused as if trying to listen to the conversation, then continued his own discussion.

"Why?" Anton hissed. He felt that old panic begin to creep into his mind. *Stop it*, he told himself. Thurgose was armed. It could handle this. That thought seemed to help, but just a little.

"We have stumbled into an illicit procedure," Thurgose said. It continued to watch the natives. "They fear we will report them." It tossed its muzzle toward the leader. "He said we are tourists and not a threat. We will leave." Anton smiled at the fellow, trying to make a good impression. He considered a wave, but his hand was trembling too much. "The other creature," Thurgose said, "prefers to eliminate any potential witness." Anton stared at the native. He was tall, but hunched over. Then, he realized. The panhandler. Was this his revenge for not getting money? Anton cursed himself for not handing over the kylacks. He should have thought ahead. They were visitors. Why make enemies? It was too late now.

"Tell them we will leave like little hutones," Anton suggested. "We will be gone tomorrow and never darken their forest again." The words sounded light, but he didn't feel that way. His heads was pounding; his breath seemed so hot.

"I suggested we leave shortly after our arrival," Thurgose noted. "That's when they started discussing our impending future."

"I can outrun them," Anton said. He was beginning to feel better. The longer they stood there, the stronger he felt. He was a Frighem, trained in defense. They were large beings, but no doubt slow.

"To where?" Thurgose asked. Anton managed a wry smile. Thurgose had simply been asking for a destination, but he recognized a secondary meaning. They would be trapped in the ship. He was carrying Thurgose's power packs in his bag. Without them, take off was impossible. The ship could still function; its defenses would handle most attacks, but only for a short time without Thurgose's guidance.

They certainly couldn't go to town. They didn't even know where it is. Back to the adobe hut? That was an idea, but it hardly seemed a great place to be inside with seven natives armed with thick knives outside. The roly-poly agent hardly seemed like a great addition to the defense.

Anton could see one of the blades glistening in the light. It was very evil looking. There was only one choice. If matters demanded, they would fight. Thurgose could kill at least four of them. He would have to handle the others as best he could.

Anton began to estimate distances to the closest worker, the ways he might grab a knife and use it. He could see himself taking brave and powerful swings, neatly slicing an attacker the way they had sliced a tree. They didn't seem concerned with the images that flashed through his mind. One was beginning to hack away at a tree in short, quick strokes, like a clock striking an hour. Another was stripping leaves off the fallen trees. There were about eight trees lying in the clearing. Their demise had crushed dozens of smaller trees. The natives, clad in thick, high boots, basically ignored those smaller ones, although occasionally plucking one or two leaves. The procedure required strength.

A native grasped a leaf where it attached to the tree and twisted as much as he could and then jerked down hard. The entire leaf would come off in his hand. At the same time, the tree spit sap at him and flung needles. More sap dripped down from the leaf end and spilled across the rich soil.

In the quiet, Anton began to hear more noises. First, there were just distant hums. Then there were louder creaks and groans. He couldn't understand. However, the workers froze and listened intently. The leader shouted, and they scrambled for the truck. All seven natives either jumped into the cab or climbed into the back where the parts of the trees were being stored. The sounds were almost on top of them. Anton looked up and saw a helicopter. It had appeared out of nowhere. There were shouts, yells, engine noises and a sudden tumult erupting everywhere.

He glanced at Thurgose, but the little creature was still trying to evaluate the situation. A shot was fired from the truck, and a beam of light struck the ground in front of them. It dug a small hole in the soil. Anton stared at it for just a moment before falling down for safety. Thurgose rolled back and forth in front of him. Its skull was deep green; its eyes, intense.

Anton kept his head down, but he could hear the sounds of firing. Creatures seemed to be pouring through the trees, oblivious to the needles and sap. At least two helicopters raced overhead. The noise continued. Shouts, screams. There was an explosion.

Anton heard footsteps. A native came stumbling into the clearing from the other side. He clutched his hand to his chest. His other hand held a black weapon. Thurgose turned to confront him. The native grinned, and Anton recognized the panhandler. He had been wounded. A liquid seeped through his fingers, mingling black with the green sap. He had apparently marched right through the trees. His leather apron was a mass of needles. His arms and head held their own share. He tripped over one of the discarded, dead trees, cursed it and kicked at it. Then he moved unsteadily toward them.

Thurgose did not hesitate, but fired his left nostril. The man was knocked backward by the blast that struck him in the middle of his chest, just below his hand. He looked down, then at the horse. He tried to raise his gun, but could not. Then, almost in slow motion, he crumpled.

"Nice shot," a voice said behind Anton. He glanced over anxiously. The agent from the hut was there. He, too, held a handgun-like weapon. He stepped around Anton and walked to the body. He turned it over and nodded.

Anton stood up and dusted himself. Then, he stopped. The agent had spoken to him in Dalian. His heart was beating so loudly he couldn't be sure, but he had understood what the agent said. Anton looked at Thurgose, but the little horse was still in its defensive posture. The green light dimmed, but did not go out. As the agent walked back, Thurgose readied himself again.

"He's dead," the agent said. This time, Anton was sure. The native had spoken in Dalian. He peered suspiciously at him. The agent seemed the same although he had reattached his suspenders. "I think we got the rest," the agent continued. There were more footsteps. Another burly native sped up and said something. The agent nodded and made a quick order. The second native ran back. Overhead, the helicopters were leaving.

Anton could hear the crunch of leaves being ground underfoot, but he was too curious now to be frightened. "Sorry you had to walk into the middle of this," the agent said.

He turned and accidently brushed into a tree. Immediately, it sank a dozen needles into his arm. The agent didn't even wince. Anton just stared. Why had he ever thought he could conquer these people? They were impervious to pain.

Thurgose kept between the agent and Anton as the three retreated down the path to the hut. "Rotten business," the agent said. He pulled out a cigarette and lit it. Anton was becoming so used to the smell; he didn't even react as the acrid smoke floated across him. He also realized he was getting very tired. Searching around the bag—itself dirt-covered and smelly—he found some more dydala and started to eat some. It, too, tasted like those trees. This brief stop was becoming a nightmare. He knew he would wake up one day and find everything bore that harsh, awful aroma. He leaned over.

"How does he know Dalian?" he asked Thurgose. "We must be their first visitors from there." The animal did not reply. Anton decided it must be thinking, too.

He pursed his lips and tried to concentrate. It was hard. There were many natives and agents in these trees and every now and then, a sharp noise interrupted his thoughts. Occasionally, someone would hurry across the path in front or behind them. Thurgose was kept busy rolling around Anton to keep him fully guarded. The agent never seemed to notice the interruptions, but kept walking and smoking.

Perhaps these people had a facility for language, Anton considered. That was possible. Or they could exchange language tapes with a Thurgose and assimilate the information quickly. Perhaps the giant computer could translate. Or they owned a universal translator that was somehow not visible. Perhaps the agent was speaking in his own Quitoan tongue, but it was being translated by some small device into Dalian. Now that was a possibility. Pleased with his ability to fathom these things out, Anton relaxed and began to skip along behind the agent. He was beginning to like the native. There was something very calm and self-assuring about him. He had an air of confidence, a surety of manner.

Anton threw back his shoulders and tried to walk in that firm, striding way. That's the way he wanted to be—strong, confident, brave. For a moment, he was sorry he did not have a cigarette dangling from his mouth. That would complete the image. Damn the smoke. It was not so foul he couldn't stand it. Nothing could affect him now.

They stopped by the hut. "Follow that road there," the agent pointed. "It's about two jargons to Friga. That should take you maybe fifteen minutes. There's a nice hotel. The energy office has been alerted, and you'll be able to get your fill in the morning. They have great frynck weeds there, too. Not like these." He held up a cigarette and frowned. "These are cheap ones. Probably wouldn't last very long in the ring."

Anton didn't ask him to explain. He was too busy admiring the man's easy style. Of course, the agent was so strong. Maybe, Anton wondered, he might grow that powerful. Of course, if he had to smoke frynck weeds to do it, he would definitely give them a try.

"And don't touch the weeds," the agent continued. "They are government property." Anton nodded. "Poachers," the agent continued. "This weed is valuable. I imagine we stopped a shipment worth forty thousand credits tonight." He glanced at Anton. "Just routine. We do this most every night. Funny, isn't it? The weeds are the only thing keeping the soil together, and these poachers keep cutting away at it. You wouldn't believe it, but this whole continent was once covered with weeds. Now we're down to a few hundred jargons of the stuff. If poachers keep it up, the frynck fights will be nothing." The agent sighed. "That's just hard to figure out." He stubbed the cigarette on the bench. "Just wound up, I guess. I shouldn't keep talking."

"How can you speak Dalian so well?" Anton finally blurted. The question kept gnawing at him.

"When your friend came in," the agent gestured at Thurgose, "we just exchanged discs. He's just better at getting the ports right than I am." He shook his head. "The damn technicians haven't solved that yet.

Anton stood there. Disc? What did the agent do, eat it? He brightened. Maybe there was a way to learn a new language without spending years studying it. Just ingest the disc. But how? "I don't understand," he finally said.

Thurgose looked up at him. "The simplest element sometimes requires the most complex solution," it quoted happily. The green light was out, but the other colors were faint. The little horse was extremely low on energy.

Anton frowned at it. "That's it," he insisted, "no more philosophy. You're getting too sarcastic."

Thurgose bowed its head. "Dalia had long been known for its philosophy. Even my builder was ingrained with it."

"Shame mine wasn't," the agent said. He undid his shirt buttons and pulled back a small tab. His chest opened to reveal a maze of wires, flywheels, microchips and other equipment. "Not an ounce of philosophy in there," he said.

"Pity," Thurgose said calmly. Anton, on the other hand, didn't have anything more to say.

VI

When the suns came up, Anton rose with them. The first appeared in the east, rising majestically the way both suns did over Dalia. For a moment, he recalled the many mornings he had bathed in the warm, ever-flowing spring outside the palace. It was a public bath. Many people came, the royal family not the least of them.

From his lofty view, Anton could also see the second sun joining the first from the north. It was far distant and offered little heat to the planet, but it was still bigger than a star and certainly closer. At noon, the two suns joined together at an apex that made that part of the day hotter than it otherwise would have been. Then, as afternoon lengthened, the distance between the suns did, too, until the morning rolled around again. Also from the bedroom window, Anton could see the small backwards town of Ilada. Named for the pioneer who founded it, Ilada had little to offer a tourist. This was the one hotel, which did a rousing business only during frynck fight time. Then, as now, all 15 rooms filled up. Actually, most tourists flew back to their homes rather than reside in this dusky, dingy community.

Anton could see most of the city simply by looking left and then right. The main street was nothing more than dirt with adobe buildings lining both sides. In case of rain, planks made from the fibers of frynck weeds were laid down so the residents could cross the street. However, they were little used. The clerk at the front desk told Thurgose the town nickname was "little aid," in a play on the words for the lack of succor in this distant locale. He told them visitors came and stayed only if they were trying to get away from civilization.

That horror was represented by the small villages on the other side of the planet. There, the weather was controlled, and everything was technologically oriented. On this side, a Quitoan could be free, the clerk said, calmly spitting frynck weed juice into a small spittoon. Not that some technology wasn't a bit handy, he added hastily. Anton decided he was referring to the closed-circuit television, the gadget that automatically registered the guests by reading the "visa" computer tape; or the escalator to the fourth floor level. Compromises had to be made, the clerk said.

Outlets allowed Anton to re-energize the power packs. They drained enough energy to dim lights across the community.

Anton had been surprised no one was interested in the night's raid. It was obviously a common event. Gazing out of his window, he thought he understood why. All the passersby resembled the poachers: rough, dirt-covered and determined. Even the female natives—sometimes distinguishable by clothing, sometimes not—had that same harshness about them.

Behind him, Thurgose made a small noise. Anton glanced over his shoulder. The little horse had put his tail into a socket as soon as they arrived. "This sensates divinely," it announced just before Anton dozed off on the hard bed. The horse was still plugged in this morning.

"Don't overdose," Anton cautioned.

Thurgose released its tail. "Brubiscon, you can't fully appreciate the pleasure such connections give me."

"Would you were as I am," Anton recited, dredging up a quote from a 15th century author, "you would understand. Since you are not, you cannot." He laughed. "I always thought there should be some concluding line like 'so forget I said anything.' That would be appropriate."

Thurgose chose to test his various functions and avoid conversations. Anton watched, almost enviously, as the little horse turned green, blue, pink, red, yellow and orange in succession, blinking like a walking rainbow. His eyes watered as he thought about the colors of Dalia. Only an artistic people would create a robot with such a palate. In Quito, everything was green or gray, colors befitting their creative temperament. Anton longed for the bright hues of home. Instead, he could just look out on this dim imitation and wonder if he would ever go home again.

His dreams were filled with reminders: visions of his father, visions of the quiet gardens, visions of the multi-colored room he used to sleep in. And visions, too, of Yani, his cousin whom he had hoped to marry someday. He had told his father and the king had winked as if he understood. Of course, nothing had come of it although he was sure she knew how he felt. Somehow, he had forgotten her. Perhaps the endless boredom, the long hours of study and the tragedy that had forced him to flee had driven her from his mind. But now she came back in the quiet of the first peaceful night he had spent on land in years. She also reminded him of the world he left behind. Since there was nothing more he could do, he closed his eyes, erased the image and opened them again to the slowly awakening Ilada. The difference was startling and very sad.

"Have you ingested anything?" Thurgose asked as its morning check was completed.

"I was thinking of trying a frynck weed," Anton teased. The smell still lingered, but was not overwhelming from this lofty spot.

"I believe I warned you about the consequences of such consumption," Thurgose said.

Anton turned in mock anger. "Take away all the fun, wouldn't you? Then it will just have to be something else. Your problem is you're just a horse-in-the-corner. I bet you'd get angry if I looked like I was happy."

"I do not know," Thurgose replied smoothly. "I've rarely seen that expression."

Anton recognized the wisdom in that and stopped kidding. The little creature did not intend to be so pointed with its comments. It just wasn't designed for that. Still, it was right. He had not been happy lately. Perhaps he should do something different, something to break the monotony before they boarded the ship and left again.

"Let's go to the frynck fights," he suggested eagerly. He was surprised by just how excited he was by the thought. He didn't even know what they were, but they might be like the wrestling matches he used to love on the video. Then he would laugh, pointing and howling at the antics of the men jumping on each other. When his father would recommend he do something a bit more educational—such as participating in the puzzles on another channel—he would slink off to his room and switch the wrestling back on. It was not a long show, but it was long enough to give him the energy for the more tedious chores. Of course, no wrestling tapes had been stocked with the other supplies. Funny, he thought, he had forgotten about that, too.

How much more was there crammed away in the dark recesses of his brain he had forgotten? It would all come spilling out when he had children. If…. Another gray cloud passed through his mind. He shut it off. Thurgose could worry about creating dynasties. For the moment, he was going to appreciate the lovely day, the two suns and the gray town.

After breakfast—a non-descript porridge that looked like a

beige piece of Quito soil, and came with beige bread and beige, hot liquid—the two Dalians stepped out into the sunlight to enjoy the morning. Already, dozens of people were on the streets going in various directions.

Anton asked Thurgose for some translations and quickly learned the location of the bank. A quick exchange—at an unknown, unarguable rate—and he had enough to pay for breakfast and his hotel room bill. The tellers were a bit taken aback by the Dalian currency, particularly since it didn't show up on their charts, but they concocted an instant exchange rate. Lacking vocabulary, Anton would have accepted anything, but Thurgose bargained. It said that was the local custom. That and spitting frynck weed juice. Everyone seemed to do that. Anton didn't need a translator to know he had to look very carefully before walking. Spittoons may have been invented, but they obviously weren't popular with everyone.

By early afternoon, he was tired of sightseeing. Thurgose was eager to leave while the light was proper for navigation, but Anton was adamant. He would stay to see the fights.

Thurgose finally gave in, but only after the power packs were carefully placed back on board and tested. Thurgose recharged himself again while Anton took a nap. The horse then test fired its weapons at a target range located outside the town. Several shooters, who were practicing with light-producing guns, stopped to watch and comment. Apparently nasal projectiles had gone out of style years before. Metal was hard to find, and with the small population, politicians ruled handguns threatened too many people. Light-producing weapons, which tended to stun, achieved prominence after that. Of course, they could be deadly if the control gauges were properly set. Anton had seen evidence of that the night before.

As the two suns grew further apart, small groups of visitors began to arrive. Anton had no trouble recognizing them. Although many were burly individuals—surprisingly cleanly dressed—most wore a matching pants and coat combination, although all wore boots. Anton, who still checked out feet, was disappointed. He had hoped someone on this planet knew the scarring technique, but they were just not that culturally advanced.

Women who arrived were well-dressed, some with small hats, but all with thick, heavy shoes. Anton found them strange looking with their few teeth that served to grind food rather than run from front to back, and their ear grooves instead of a simple hole. He was beginning to notice other differences: extra folds around the neck, double lids over the eyes and a less useful thumb. It had little ability to rotate, but seemed locked in place. Also, the women were much prettier on Dalia. Their skin had been brighter, more translucent so colors underneath appeared. Women here were thick-skinned. Their faces were also less appealing. They, in turn, seemed unconcerned by his presence.

Later, as dozens of tourists from other planets arrived, he understood why. There were people with wings, or talons, who walked on four legs or who had to wear air tanks. None looked remotely like Dalians. As he surveyed the strange visitors, Anton realized why Thurgose had chosen Quito as their stopping place. The two of them would fit in regardless of their appearance.

Towards late afternoon, the crowds began to migrate down the main street toward a small arena on the edge of the city. From the hotel room, it resembled a tiny bowl set into the landscape. Now, mingling with the others who shuffled, hopped, walked or marched, Anton realized the facility was much bigger than it looked.

The many feet threw up great clouds of choking dust which mingled with a dozen perfumes from as many planets. Through it all, weaving back and forth around everyone, ran the smell of frynck weeds. Some smoked what they carried. A few stopped to purchase cigarettes from young vendors. The youngsters had them stuffed into pockets and sidled through the throng, whispering and surreptitiously taking money. Anton just shook his head whenever one of the boys came near. That was enough to dissuade them.

Lines formed in front of three ticket booths, but the tellers inside worked quickly. Thurgose ordered the tickets; Anton paid by simply emptying his pockets. The clerk gave him a disgusted look, took enough and left the rest. They then followed the crowd inside.

They emerged on the top level, which was the fifth row from the center. The arena was round, but the center ring was rectangular. Three strands of a rope-like material guarded the ring. There was a stool in one corner. Guards stood by the first row, preventing anyone from sitting there, but all of the other seats were available. Anton gestured toward a vacant pair in the middle of the third row, and they threaded their way to them. The noise was constant around them, the hubbub of a dozen languages mingling with the cries of youngsters selling programs and assorted snacks.

One vendor carried a tray near Anton, and he glanced at it. The young Quitoan was carrying something that looked like a rock with soft globules on it. Naturally, the whole thing was beige. Thurgose offered to test it, but Anton opted for the remaining dydala in his bag. He may have been a little hungry, but he just wasn't ready for that local cuisine. He watched grimly as a neighbor purchased the treat, crammed it into his mouth and bit down with a sudden unhinging of his large jaws. The result was a loud, startling crunch. The man chewed contently with a blissful look on his face. Anton managed to avoid gagging.

Thurgose checked the program and then handed it to the Anton. It consisted of pictures of five individuals, all bare-chested and grim. Each carried a large blade, akin to the kind the poachers had, but thinner. It looked very dangerous. Each picture was accompanied by the competitor's record and titles, which Thurgose translated. This night, the most important champion was scheduled to appear to defend his ranking. That had drawn the overflow crowd. Seats were quickly filled, and ticketholders began to sift into the aisles and line up behind the last row. Others continued to buy tickets, although they must have been only able to see heads of those standing from the outside. The vendors certainly didn't stop selling tickets.

Anton began to feel extremely claustrophobic. He decided that was the result of the trip. He simply wasn't used to so many people. He edged closer to Thurgose as spectators created seats by filling in the bare inches left vacant on any bench.

The din increased until it was overwhelming. Anton was obligated to put hands over his ear holes to protect his sensitive hearing. The hulking native next to him said something, and Thurgose, who was now a pale green and overwhelmed by the many scents and sounds, translated that he was offering a bet on the first bout. Anton politely refused. The native eyed him and said something else.

"It's a tradition to bet," Thurgose explained.

"I don't want to offend him," Anton hissed, "but it's a tradition on my planet not to be a sucker. I'll bet on the second match." Thurgose relayed that message, and that seemed to satisfy the native. A garrulous type, he then launched into an explanation of the event.

From what Thurgose could comprehend, the matches had been going on since the earliest explorations. The Quito government was trying to stop the bouts in an effort to preserve the frynck weeds and the local top soil, but not too strenuously. There was an immense income generated by foreign tourists. So the fights continued.

At the same time, locals got rich reporting when raids would take place on the local frynck weed patches. Anton nodded at that. The panhandler was probably caught in the act. No wonder he had reacted so directly. He probably thought Thurgose and Anton would identify him to the agent. At least his behavior was explained.

His companion wanted to keep talking, but there was a sudden buzz through some sort of loudspeaker system. Anton couldn't see anything but he certainly heard it. Later, he realized his seat was wired. With the buzz—a harsh, raucous noise that befitted the occasion—the crowd quieted. There was a hum as someone carried a small frynck weed plant into the ring.

It was a miniature compared to the trees, but looked just as dangerous. It sat in a large beige pot and was placed in the right corner across from the stool.

An announcer slipped through the ropes and stood in the center. He pointed at a far aisle and shouted something. Immediately, a cheer went up as someone ran through those standing along the route. Trim and powerful looking, he jumped into the ring and ran around it, holding the stick up in his hand and waving it. The native next to Anton said something.

"He's undefeated," Thurgose reported.

"At running through crowds?" Anton asked. He stopped Thurgose from translating that. There was no reason to let his seatmate in on the sarcasm.

The fighter had several companions who patted his shoulders and rubbed something on to his face. Then they got out of the ring and stood below. The weed also had someone with it. He held a small fan and tested it by turning it off and on away from the plant.

There was another buzz, and the cheering began again. The fighter approached the plant carefully as if examining it. He shifted quickly from spot to spot. Behind the plant, the man with the fan imitated the fighter. As the fighter neared, the man turned the fan on. The blast of air struck the weeds left front near the top and activated a sudden burst of needles. The fighter simply leaped aside and the needles struck the ground harmlessly. The crowd roared. That continued for several more seconds: the fighter edging in; the plant firing needles and missing.

Then, in a sudden move almost too quick to see, the fighter swung his stick and then sprinted away. He had to move quickly as the plant spat sap at him from its damaged side. The man's attack was a good one, for the weed began to list. It did not topple, but it had been cut badly. Sap oozed down its side in a great stream, bubbling out rapidly.

The crowd shouted its approval. The man next to Anton rose to his feet, clapping. Others dotted around the arena imitated him.

In a moment, there was another buzz, and the sweaty fighter retreated to his corner. His handler emerged to towel him off, give him water and counsel him. A minute later, the second round began. This time, the plant succeeded in hitting the fighter with some needles. The crowd gasped; the man next to Anton groaned and nervously felt the wad of bills in his pocket. Sap dripped from the wound. The fighter staggered away, and the plant kept firing. In a few moments, the fighter was covered with needles.

The shift had been so sudden, Anton had been startled. He really couldn't believe anyone would fight a weed, but he was positively astounded the weed could win.

The second round ended with the fighter in trouble. The third and fourth rounds were slower. The plant's needle supply seemed low; the fighter was still recovering. His handlers had removed the needles, but the green sap mixed with dark blood.

The weed was not in good shape either. The initial cut had sealed, but the top half of the plant now listed at almost a 70 degree angle. In addition, there were smaller cuts all over it and two leaves had been hacked completely off.

Anton, beginning to be caught up in the excitement, was sorry he had not bet something. He liked the plant. It showed more class than the fighter. For one thing, it hadn't pranced about before the fight, and it didn't move during it. It received no water like the fighter and was not toweled off. Its handler did slip away for a drink, but the plant remained, firm, resolute, ready. Anton admired that.

In the fifth round, however, the fighter got the upper hand. Quick slashes with the skla, and another leaf fell. The plant was almost defenseless on the left side. The fighter moved in, disregarded a short burst of sap and defiantly sliced off the top third of the weed. The rest followed, accompanied by the cheers of the throng. Anton's companion almost shouted himself hoarse. He pounded Anton on the back in ecstasy.

The fighter waved to the crowd and leaped the ropes with new found vigor. He danced up the aisle as people reached over to pat his back, say something or look in awe at his many welts.

"Can a plant kill someone?" Anton asked when the noise level dropped.

Thurgose checked. "He said it has happened. The needles are not venomous, nor is the sap. However, in combination, in a weakened state, a fighter can go into shock."

"The audience, too," Anton murmured. He was reminded of his second bout promise and reluctantly bet on the man. And won. The fighter, a tall, skinny native, easily dispatched the plant with a sudden thrust as opposed to a sweep. The skla pierced the plant about midway and allowed most of the sap to drop out. It was a quick, savage blow. Weakened, the plant was unable to hurl its needles far enough to defend itself and was quickly dispatched. So it went for two more fights.

Anton developed an admiration for the stick. It didn't seem like much, but a skla in the right hands turned out to be a deadly weapon with surprisingly razor-sharp edges.

Now night crept over the arena. Lights planted in the ground and under the center ring fought back the shadows. Excitement grew along with the darkness. The champion was coming. The ring was cleaned for the fourth time by men on their knees. A hush fell over the crowd. Anton waited with the rest. He knew where to look now. In the far corner, there was a beige curtain over an exit. When it opened, a fighter always entered. Suddenly, it parted.

The emerging native was taller than the other fighters and wearing a purple cloak. That alone made him stand out. It was the first breath of color Anton recalled seeing. The champion stood for a moment by the entrance as if accepting the homage of the crowd. Then, surrounded by his handlers, he began to move forward. The mass of bodies moved together, forcing room in the crowds. In the middle, barely able to move his legs, the champion seemed relaxed and content. He held his head erect. Almost unconsciously, Anton imitated him. They were erect together, confident together. Anton felt energy roaring through his veins. He was almost ready to take the skla stick himself and dash into the ring. What a puny plant to challenge such a being.

The champion reached the ring. Anton could see him now as he jumped up and down to warm up. The muscles were clearly defined in his shoulders. Here and there were ridges. Anton nodded. Scars. They may not be on his feet, but the champion had them. Now they were getting to the real adults in this culture. There was such fluidity in the fighter's moves, ease in his face. He was completely bald, making his ear grooves seem to stand out. He took the cloak and folded it neatly. It was a simple, yet powerful gesture.

Anton elbowed the native next to him; not a difficult feat considering how close they were. "Want to bet?" he asked. He had already learned the Quitoan word for betting. The native nodded. Anton pointed at the champion and then himself. His champion shrugged. Feeling in his pocket, Anton found he had eight coins left. He pulled them out. The Quitoan smiled appreciably. They touched knees on the wager. Anton had picked up that custom quickly, too. When he looked up, a giant frynck weed was in the ring. It was bigger and taller than the previous four combined. The champion had to sneer up at it. Anton could see he wasn't fazed by the obstacle. His companion said something.

"He is an old fighter," Thurgose reported. "Your friend said he is supposed to retire in rapid time."

Old, Anton sniffed. Look at him. The champion was in impressive condition. Old? Just a bettors' ploy. In this case, it wouldn't matter. Anton had no more money. He wished he had. Old? He'd bet his kingdom on such a fighter.

The large frynck required twos native with fans. Each guarded a different side. The fans were bigger, too. In his corner, the champion waved his arms and practiced his thrusts. He seemed smaller compared to his opponent, but none the weaker. Again, the crowd grew quiet. There was a yell from the side and some laughter. Then, silence. The buzz to start the fight seemed so loud.

The champion swaggered to the center and faced the plant. He made a few playful thrusts and smiled as the throng applauded. The plant's seconds held their fans and waited. In a lightening move, the champion suddenly moved in, cut and backed away. In reaction, needles and sap fell far short. Anton was both astounded and delighted by the speed. Old? The champ had the grace of any dancer he had ever seen on Dalia. And there were many dancers on his home planet.

The champ had hit his mark, too. The middle frond was barely attached. The sap flow stopped quickly. This was an older tree. Unlike the young ones, it had experience in staunching wounds.

Anton held his breath as the champion raced in again, cut and slashed and fled as quickly as before. Again, needles and sap failed to touch him. Anton's companion groaned and shouted something at the plant.

"He wants the plant to be more responsive," Thurgose told Anton. The little horse's green light had gone out before, but now it was back on. Anton noticed it, but was too interested in the fight to comment. He was on his feet along with hundreds of others to cheer when the round ended.

The champion sat on his stool. Anton was surprised to see how much his chest rose and fell. He was breathing much too hard for such limited movement. However, the frynck weed had suffered greatly in those first few minutes. It would not be long now.

The second round was a duplicate of the first except the champion did not exit quite as rapidly. He received several needles into his shoulder. His assistants did not try to remove them. These were not immature needles, but long, pointed ones that dug in deeply. Anton saw the champion wince.

He shouted to urge him on, silently offering to give his energy to the fighter. He concentrated and tried to direct the force of his being toward the champion. He used to do that while watching wrestling, and the beneficiary sometimes seemed to respond. Anton was willing to try. Yet he realized the champion could not survive a long fight. He was older, and he was losing strength rapidly. Dark blood rolled down his arms and created a strange pattern on his light skin. Sweat glistened on his scalp and droplets cascaded down his nose. His face had lost some of its determination.

Even from afar, Anton could tell the champion's eyes were no longer fixed and forceful. Yet, when the buzzer went, the warrior rose from his stool, took a firm grip on the skla between his second and third fingers, and marched across the ring.

In the previous rounds, the frynck had waited for the champion to make the first move. This time, it struck first. Both fans acted at once to activate the plant. Needles flew across the open space accompanied with sap. The force struck the champion full in the chest. Sap dripped from the end of each needle. The champion staggered backwards, only getting his balance when he reached the ropes. He looked down at his chest and became angry. His face darkened, and he bit his lower lip. Getting firmly to his feet, he eyed the plant. He edged sideways to reduce his own target area and then picked up the pace. A second later, a frond floated in the air and fell to a chorus of cheers. There had been a gasp when the champion had been hit, but like him, the crowd recovered.

Thurgose tried to get Anton's attention, but the prince was too excited to notice him. Another swift move by the champion, and a second frond joined the first on the mat.

Quitoan and weed stood inches apart in the center of the ring and hurried their best shots at each other. The champion hacked away at the trunk; the plant fired volley after volley of needles. When the buzzer finally rang, both were in tatters. The champion staggered back to his stool, his body a mass of needles. Sap had discolored his light purple trunks and cascaded across his knee-high boots. The weed had lost a foot of trunk from its top. Four fronds were cut; sap gushed from several severe cuts.

Thurgose finally grabbed Anton's arm with its mouth. Anton whirled angrily. "Look," the horse said. It had to shout to be heard. Anton glanced upward and gaped. There was Wyron's ship, still far away, but clearly visible in the night sky. It had its landing lights on, playing up the red frame. "We cannot abide," Thurgose said. It began to edge down the aisle. Anton reluctantly followed.

They were halfway across when the next round began. Anton tried to stop. His betting partner had realized he was leaving and was coming, too, shouting something. The champion was moving wobbly into the center of the ring. The plant was already firing. There were loud groans and shouts from the crowd.

Anton was pushed by people. He almost caromed out into the aisle, there to fall over more legs and bodies. Thurgose was still in front, worming through the crowds. There were cheers. Anton tried to turn to see, but couldn't. He tried to guess from the noises, but there were so many. The heavy boots were close behind him. Just over the great trees beyond, Wyron was coming. Thurgose was pulling at him. Anton was lost, confused, crying, yelling. His voice was nothing in the massive roars and shouts around him. They stumbled out. The native Anton bet with was right behind, still shouting. He was so round; however, he was almost totally entangled in the spectators jammed in every available space.

Suddenly, Anton and Thurgose were free and running. Behind them, like a giant wave, sound roared over the walls of the arena. It washed across them. Anton wanted to turn back, but he knew he couldn't. Heart aching, he raced beside Thurgose. The little horse was picking up speed. Its skull was dark green now. Power had turned its body an array of colors. They sped down the main street.

It was virtually deserted. A couple of lanterns hanging in windows were the only lights.

Anton was breathing heavily by the time they approached the ship. He could still hear the noise from the arena. It was fainter now. He hoped it didn't mean the champion had lost. Impatiently, Thurgose activated the elevator, and they rode the few feet to the airlock and bolted the door behind them. Thurgose rolled to the controls while Anton reconnected the elevator and closed the outer sheath. He sprinted to his seat and put the belt on. The engines were already going. The craft shuttered. Thurgose was talking to someone in the control tower. It was arguing strenuously. Anton could barely hear as the blood roared through his brain. Looking quickly to the screen, he could see the Kajan ship clearly. It was but a few miles away and closing. Was Thurgose being told not to take off until it landed?

He closed his eyes and took a deep breath. He could barely think. They had to get out of here. Their rear weaponry was useless if Wyron chose to attack. Maybe the Kajan hadn't seen them. That was possible. It was an old ship. Maybe. Damn the maybes. Anton strained to look at Thurgose. The little horse was firm. It cut off communications and thrust the liftoff button. There was a great burst of energy. The ship shuddered and started away.

"We are hit, Brubiscon," Thurgose said. Its voice was barely audible over the engines.

"Are we in trouble?"

"No," Thurgose repeated. "We have been assailed in our rear compartment. At this moment, I do not know if the Kajan ship fired upon us or if the matter is a control method from ground." The ship was rapidly pulling away from the Kajan vessel and Quito. Anton tried to see the arena, but it was just a blur. Everything was just a blur. The force of the takeoff pushed him back into the cushioned seat and held him. For the first time, he was glad he didn't have to do anything. He felt totally drained.

Thurgose checked the various gauges. "Can we continue?" Anton asked wearily. His voice was reluctant to come out.

"Yes," the horse answered. "Damage appears to be to the major energy circuit."

"What does that mean?"

"We can fly, but not far. We are currently operating on power packs alone."

Anton shivered. They couldn't outmaneuver the Kajan now.

They wouldn't even be able to outfly him. If they did not seek land and repairs, at some point, they would be helpless in space. The Wyron could attack at his leisure. Or not attack. They would drift until food and air…Anton stopped. His tired mind didn't want to think, but he forced it.

"Let's go back."

Thurgose considered that. "We would have to avoid Wyron. I can take evasive action. The natives here are sufficiently technologically advanced to help."

Anton sighed. "But Wyron won't have to find us again. We'll be right there."

"Yes."

"Then we must go on." There would be no point in going back to Quito. Wyron could do as he wanted. Certainly he didn't know the language or the customs, but there was no guarantee he would be unable to bribe the appropriate officials or do what would have to be done before repairs could be made.

"Could we fight?" Anton suggested.

"Without sufficient energy, we could manage a few antipersonnel salvos, but the effect would drain us," Thurgose said.

"Can we make it back to the place where they speak English?" Anton tried. That was where he was supposed to go in the first place.

"Our possibilities are good," Thurgose said.

"Then we will." Anton closed his eyes as the ship headed into space. He felt like the old fighter, very tired and very sore, but having nothing else to do but to wade once more into the center of the ring. Sleep slipped up on him. He fought it for just a moment.

Behind the golden ship and its sleeping crew, the red vessel of Kajan turned slowly and began to follow at a leisurely pace.

VII

Lynard Orlando leaned forward on his desk, looked over his glasses at the sole occupant in the waiting room and furrowed his brow. The man, meticulously dressed in a crisp suit with perfect seams, glanced at him, paled and looked away. Orlando did not smile, but inside, he was delighted. He could get his brow to look like tilled soil on an Iowa farm. That took practice, but he had plenty of time to practice. A lot of people came to this waiting room. They had to for their 10-year evaluation. Orlando did not have much more to do than sit there and make them very uncomfortable. His job actually was simply to note the scheduled individual had arrived, check over the electronic forms to be sure they were complete and then record when the person left.

It was a position perfectly suited for someone with no desire for a 3 rating. But Orlando was not satisfied with shuffling paper and watching the clock slowly mark the passing of his day. So he wrinkled his forehead and scowled a lot. The people who came to this small, simple waiting room had no idea why he was there. They would see him sitting behind the desk and assume he was intimately connected to the evaluation that lay ahead. He certainly had no desire to do anything to dissuade them. He had developed an excellent scowl.

Orlando had seen it on an older man who had left the evaluation room before time had elapsed. Enchanted by the grim, forceful appearance, Orlando had screwed up his lips and directed his gaze into a mirror for days before becoming satisfied with what he saw. He picked up a sheet of paper and put on his best scowl. The man in the chair almost winced while Orlando applauded himself—silently, of course.

He did not know the man in the room. The e-form he received contained limited data, but, out of boredom and wanting to let his scowling, furrowing muscles rest a moment, he scanned the sheet. The man was a Walter Marson Canyon, a civilian assigned to the military base in Phoenix. Orlando looked up from his computer and cocked an eyebrow as if surprised by something he had read. Canyon turned a lovely shade of red, squirmed uneasily and tried to pretend he wasn't paying attention.

Occasionally, one of his victims would wander over and ask Orlando what exactly was wrong. The clerk hated that. He did not like being on the defensive. It was much more fun undermining the confidence of people who could someday become a 3. He couldn't tell by just looking who would succeed. Besides, no one ever told him everything. He had to scan the electronic newspaper when the announcements were made. Then he never remembered the names anyway. Still, he could usually tell if a particular person was a hopeless case. Canyon fell into that category.

He was sitting stiffly, as if he had sewn wood slats into his dark suit. Everything was just so: the length of his shirtsleeve, his hair. The man looked as though he had even carefully plucked his nose hairs. Orlando scanned another line on the form—the one with the address—and shook his head. Canyon, again, feigned he was checking the wood paneling or the color picture of the moon framed high on the wall across from him. But Orlando knew. He could see Canyon's eyes shifting every now and then for a quick glance. He again furrowed his brow deeply, shook his head and made a couple of tsk, tsk noises.

That wasn't quite the full treatment, but it was close. He was sure sweat was starting under that suit. Perhaps, if there was enough time, Canyon would start to itch. Then he'd have to think of a non-embarrassing way to scratch without spoiling his appearance. Orlando had that gleeful thought behind a somber glare. There wasn't a graceful way. He just couldn't wait to see Canyon try.

He read a little further down the sheet. The gentleman had only a few years of experience, had moved up steadily. Presumably, his ratings had gone up, too. That wasn't recorded. No one trusted Orlando with that information. He knew that. At least he wasn't an Outsider.

He arched his eyes to see over the paper then quickly returned to the sheet before Canyon could react. He just might crack and become an Outsider. A man that stiff had little flexibility, and when the pressure got too strong, he might just escape from it all and live in the forests and deserts away from civilization. Orlando had heard there were a lot of people now in small camps out there. He smiled. It was a brief aberration. The thought lingered, though. Just a few of them might be there—in strange clothing, eating their meager supplies and talking gibberish—because of what he did to them in this office. It almost made everything worthwhile. And everyone said only a 3 can make an impact. Little did they know. His sister was trying to become a 3, working like crazy day and night to succeed. And all he did was sit at his desk for five hours a day and drive people crazy.

He peeked at Canyon. He was very nervous now. He was trying to hold his hands rigidly on his lap, but he couldn't stop his fingers from twitching. Orlando was sure he could see sweat budding on the top of that properly thin collar. The man was ready for the coup de grace.

Orlando set himself for the complete treatment. He called it his "total." He would grimace, put down the paper, turn his brow into that fresh cornfield look, stare over his glasses and just glare for at least 15 seconds, the victim usually tried not to look back. Then the sweat started; finally, composure would disintegrate. For just a few seconds, Lynard Orlando held a man's soul in his hands. That was so satisfying. No 3 ever did that.

He readied himself like an actor getting set to go on stage, checking himself mentally to be sure he was ready. He forced himself to scan the rest of the page slowly. Canyon would note that. They always did. Then Canyon would start thinking about any omissions he might have made or any misspellings or other silly mistakes. In just a moment, the thought would cross his mind he had failed even before he entered the dreaded computer room for the actual test. His heart would start going crazy. Sometimes, a victim would grip the armrests on the chair so tightly his hands would whiten to the color of his face. Orlando reached the bottom. He was ready for the Total. Slowly, deliberately, savagely, he put the paper down, carefully made his knuckles slap against the desk top. Canyon almost jumped.

Simultaneously, a small red light went on over the door leading to the computer room. Orlando directed his snarl towards it, but the light did not mind. Someday, Orlando vowed silently, he'd get that damn light to crumple, too. He smiled at Canyon. The effect was almost eerie, it was that different. He cleared his throat.

"You may go in, Mr. Canyon," he said calmly as if nothing had happened.

~ * ~

Canyon stood up. He stiffened his back and ran a hand over his coat to smooth it. He nodded slightly at the clerk. He had no idea what he had messed up on the form. The clerk had not said anything, but obviously something was amiss. Canyon was resigned to failure by now. For a month, everything had gone wrong. Just for starters, he had taken another hit in the ratings while Sinone continued to rise markedly.

His new assistant, Cataline, turned out to be a vivacious young woman who had already a small cadre of admirers. She was making his life miserable by smiling and eagerly carrying out every assignment well. That woman was after his job, Canyon decided, as if that were a novelty. He had been around too long not to recognize the signs. And then the appointment came for the evaluation.

He had been expecting it, but he had opened his e-mail with a trembling hand. Had 10 years passed so quickly? While he was here, fumbling with a damn form, his assistants were back in the office proving they could run everything smoothly. The road to the 3 was not paved with soft boulders. He took a deep breath. What could the evaluating computer do that wasn't being done to him already? He was about to find out.

He walked forward and seized the handle of the door. He did not look at the clerk. He just didn't think he could stand another look at the furrowed brow. The ridges were so high, Canyon half expected to see tiny people crawl out and stick miniature flags into their crests.

The office handle was cold and hard. It turned easily. There was total darkness inside. He felt his mouth go dry as he strained to see. Looking down, he realized there were tiny specks of light creating a path. He closed the door behind him. It sealed with an ominous click. The lights became brighter. He followed the path. Even before his first step was completed, he wondered if he should wait. Perhaps he was being tested for impatience. Of course, the computer might opt for a little self-determination—this time. The path was difficult to follow, but he managed to wind through about 35 steps.

Suddenly, there was a deep, hollow voice coming from beyond and above him. "Please be seated," it said.

He almost panicked. There was no seat. Should he sit on the floor? Surely, the voice didn't expect people to sit on the floor. He looked around, but the room was still pitch black. Think, he told himself. There had to be a chair somewhere. He edged backwards and immediately was rewarded by something hitting the back of his leg. Feeling behind, he found the chair and sat. It was comfortable, and he felt as though he had won a small victory. That helped erase a little bit of the 15 tortuous minutes in that waiting room.

"Please rest your arms on the side of the chair and bring your legs into contact with the plate between the chair's legs." The voice said. It was not a cold voice, more of a masculine, authoritative one. Not like Seavers either, but with a gentleness to it as if the speaker wanted to put him at ease. He moved his arms and brought his legs back even with the chair. He could feel the metal plate. He knew what they were for. Their electrodes would record all nerve impulses. There were two more on the chair's arms. They would do the same thing. Standard procedure. Still, it felt good to know what was happening. He just wished he could see.

"Welcome to your evaluation, Mr. Canyon. You will be placed in a designated situation. Please respond naturally. Your reactions will allow the computer to assess your proper status on the ranking graph." That was it. Simple, short, but what ominous meaning was left between the lines. If he failed, like Seavers, he would have a nice party and be shuffled to some small, remote position where he could do an unimportant job, and never have a chance for a 3 rating unless something incredible happened. Amazing things had happened to others. It could happen. He knew that. It was a pleasant thought at a time like this, the only pleasant one he had.

The room was not cold. Canyon could not hear anything. He also couldn't feel anything. No sense of the room closing in. He didn't expect to be scared. That would be inappropriate for the computer. He thought he would be asked questions. He did not know for sure. Few people talked about the experience. There were many for the computer to choose from anyway, Most just wanted to forget it and move on to other matters.

Canyon had seen a few people back at headquarters after their evaluation, and had longed to walk over and talk to them, but couldn't. They might have said something, but it would have spoiled his image to ask for advice. So he had walked by with a firm pace, his questions unasked and unanswered.

"Please state your name."

Canyon complied. His voice quavered a moment, but he covered that flaw quickly. Still, he wished it sounded better. His voice had an annoying habit of getting higher under stress. He fought that tendency, but he could hear a hint of squeakiness and cleared his throat to halt it. He was then asked for his address, age and current job position. He hesitated only a moment to be sure he heard the complete question before responding. He did not want any mistakes. Nor did he want to rush into a response. Let the computer see he was a careful, reasoned person. Image, he told himself. That was important.

He became aware of lights. There were many of them, racing by. Suddenly, he could see himself from above. He was seated in a large box that was moving through an endless stream of three-dimensional boxes. He watched as his box floated through waves of red and green lights across waves of hills. There was a sense of motion under his feet as he both felt the movement and saw it from above.

"You are within your own small zone," the voice said. "You are one among billions." There were shadows in every box now: some were standing; some were sitting. Each was confined by the array of lights. "You are one in this time, this place." More boxes appeared, diving from existing boxes extending on like an accordion opening up. Shadows filled them, too. "You are here. You are not here," the voice said. "There is no here or there or anywhere. There is no moment, no place, no time." Canyon began to get sleepy. He felt a gentle caress of air on his wrists, moving slowly up his arm under his shirt. It soothed him. His pulse slowed.

"You are not confined to this area, not limited to this box," the computer intoned as the walls disappeared. He could see himself moving away, walking across the nonexistent line between his space and the one inhabited by a shadow next to him. His eyes were closed—he was sure of that—but he could still see everything very clearly.

"You are on the moon. Feel the cold, hard soil."

It was there when he bent down. It scraped across his hand. The chill of the air ripped through his uniform. For a moment, he cursed the control board for not adjusting the thermostat. His office was always…. He stopped. His office wasn't on the moon. The idea disappeared in a moment.

"You are here as a soldier. You are here to guard the very important scientific equipment." Nonsense, he thought. The stuff is worthless. It's only valuable because it is here. "You must guard the outer sector. You must begin your rounds."

"I'm going," he said. He began to walk. The ground was hard here inside the underground section. Yet the light atmosphere kept him bouncing. It was too expensive to equalize pressure. Soldiers on the moon learned to adjust. He kicked away a small stone and watched it scamper far away. His mind was clear. Another day, one day closer to when he could go home.

Suddenly, there was something in front of him. The figures were fuzzy. There must have been four people, maybe more. They were descending from a platform and gathering together at least a few hundred yards away.

"Sergeant," a voice boomed. "Radar has detected a ship in your area."

Canyon winced at the sound. The voice was authoritative, and it was addressing him. He pressed down on the radio transmitter. "Yes, sir." He peered over a large rock at the distant people. "I copy four individuals," he whispered. The moon was hard and cold against his legs. Questions flooded him. How did anyone get inside the air bubble? His relief was not due for months.

"How far away?"

"A couple of football fields," Canyon estimated. "Any idea who they are?"

"Negative." There were several clicks, and the voice faded out. It returned quickly before Canyon could panic. Long nights alone sometimes led to sudden mirages, but this was different. Those people were out there. Something inside his head was trying to communicate with him, but he refused to lose concentration. He could feel the laser-gun against his thigh. If necessary, he would use it. These could be anyone. Even aliens. That thought sent chills through him. "They have been traced to a vehicle coming from extraterrestrial sources," the voice reported. Canyon's first reaction was disbelief. Base had to be kidding.

"Roger," he said out of habit.

"Use caution."

"Roger." He almost laughed. He wasn't going to throw a welcome party for these strangers. He watched them carefully. They seemed to be conferring. The largest was gesturing. There would be a full report. If this was a gag, those jokers at base were not going to get away with it. He was just supposed to monitor equipment measuring distances between stars and trying to pick up sounds emanating from deep space. That was all. If everything worked properly, scientists would be able to verify earthbound instruments. A simple assignment for a sergeant who wanted some duty off-Earth and a hefty bonus. Now this. Canyon gritted his teeth. All right. He would get ready. He scurried back inside the cave and found one of the heavy air guns. They would blast anyone who came close without seriously hurting them. He put that to his left. Now he had an option.

"Any movement?" the voice said.

Canyon peeked again. "Yes," he reported. They were walking slowly towards him. Two had stayed behind. A small one and a large one were coming closer. They were still too far away to see their features, but they looked human. They stood on two legs and clearly had arms. They were not wearing any air tanks, but did have coverings over their nose holes, like breathing tubes. They appeared a soft yellow with on occasional burst of pink and green. The small one changed colors frequently; the large ones did not.

Apparently they could climb because they had descended the ladder to the cave. Canyon considered their presence. Funny he hadn't seen them through the Plexiglas surface. Perhaps they had come from the side, landed and had never crossed the glass. Or, better yet, perhaps they had intentionally avoided the glass so he couldn't see the insignia on their ship. No matter. They were here.

His mind raced on. Did they want to seize the instruments? They were unique, but hardly that valuable. Food? There wasn't that much. Just enough for him for two more months. Military control? Possible, but no help against the Earth. This was all on the edge of the moon away from the planet. Only satellites in space made radio communication possible. He would have to see what they did, then decide.

The two coming towards his position were now less than 100 yards away. They walked stiffly as if frightened. He reported what was happening.

"Do you want to shoot?" the voice asked.

"I don't know," Canyon admitted. Panic was rising inside him. His shoulder hurt. He could see one was carrying what could be a handgun. He didn't want to die on the moon. And if he took a wild shot and blew a hole in the glass, he would die soon for lack of air. He tensed up. His muscles ached from his stiff position.

The beings were only 50 yards away. He wanted to leave, but couldn't. This was a small area. They could find him. The two were talking to each other. Canyon strained to see them. No ears. Odd-shaped eyes, bulging away from their faces. No exterior noses. The male had facial hair. Long, narrow mouths running up and down. Canyon felt his stomach bubble. Aliens. The first verified contact with aliens. Would they hurt him? What was he supposed to do?

"Aliens," he blurted into the radio. His voice was too loud. It carried to the two less than 40 feet away. They stopped and gestured toward him. One touched a black square box on his belt.

Something squawked. Canyon listened. He shook the radio. The sound came from the aliens. Were they trying to speak to him? A crazy idea interrupted his thinking. If they actually said "Take me to your leader," he wouldn't understand it.

He stood up. The smaller alien backed away. Its partner stood there. The box squawked again. Canyon shrugged and held his hands out. The aliens moved closer. The one with the box extended it toward him, as if offering it.

"What do you want?" Canyon tried. His voice did not sound very authoritative. He picked up his radio. One of the aliens pointed at it. That seemed to relax them as if they recognized it.

They said something back to him totally unintelligible. He unholstered his gun and held it out so they could see it. To scare them away. They were dangerous. He could feel that idea taking hold. Their faces frightened him. What if they had special abilities? What if they took him captive? Maybe they could shoot him from where they were. He felt dizzy and tried to steady himself. There was certainly nothing about this in the regulations.

"Get out of here!" he shouted. That was better. They looked at him, apparently startled. Maybe he had been too loud. Maybe they would get angry. Another thought entered his mind. Shouldn't he try to greet them? Perhaps they were friendly, looking for help. How could he help them? Maybe they needed fuel. There was excess oil in supply for heat and to run the generator. He could get more. They might use that. He was beginning to feel very exposed standing up. Again, they tried to say something, but he couldn't understand. He felt absolutely helpless.

They moved closer. He could see they were small, the biggest perhaps five feet tall. The tiniest one was only two feet off the ground. They were dressed in sandals and light-colored suits. The suit looked to be greenish gold.

The aliens stopped about 15 feet away. They discussed the situation with each other while Canyon watched. He could feel sweat cascading down his face. His hand tightened on the gun. If they did anything suspicious, he would shoot. What else could he do? He straightened his back. At least they would know a *United States Army*

Soldier was disciplined. For a few seconds, they faced each other across a gap of a few feet and eons of communication.

Finally, the smaller one came forward almost timidly. He put his right hand down with its back facing Canyon. It looked back to his companion for advice when that evoked no response. Canyon watched. Should he duplicate the gesture? Should he confront them? The tall one started to move toward him.

"Stop," Canyon shouted. He deliberately raised the gun and pointed it. There was no mistaking that gesture. The little one backed away and joined its partner. They moved back, keeping their eyes firmly on Canyon. Watching them go released his pent up anxiety. "Go," he shouted. He waved his left arm. "Go." Carefully aiming, he fired a shot into the ground in front of them. They ran. The light beam threw up dust.

"Sergeant," the voice said next to him.

"They are leaving," Canyon reported.

"Are you all right?"

Canyon paused. He smiled. Why not add a little icing to this one. The aliens were rapidly climbing the ladder. "Affirmative. A small wound."

"Bullet?"

"Negative," he gasped. He might as well play the part. He sagged back against the rock. "There were a lot of them, sir," he said. He picked up a nearby stone and jammed it into his left arm. It hurt. A drop of blood appeared. He stuck his finger in the rent and slightly tore his uniform. He began breathing hard. "I had to fire," Canyon reported.

"Did you hit anyone?"

"Negative."

"Have the aliens left?"

"Roger."

"Can you send us a fix on their position?"

"Negative." Canyon leaned back against the wall. He breathed heavily into the transmitter. "My arm is beginning to stiffen. I may have trouble moving."

"Roger. We will send assistance. It will be four days at least. The supply ship is not loaded. Your relief is not ready to fly."

Canyon smiled. Four days. That would be long enough to create havoc in this area. He looked around. What instrument should he destroy? Something valuable. That would enhance the desperate nature of his situation. "I think the telescope has been damaged," he reported.

"How?"

"During the fight. Possible I hit it. Or they did. I will investigate when I can."

"Roger." Canyon heard the concerned note. This was going to be interesting. He lay back and put the transistor down. Time for a nap. There would be time enough for mayhem later. "Sergeant," the voice said. "Sergeant," it repeated. Over and over again.

The lights were back. They rolled through Canyon's mind. Again, he could see himself seated in the chair.

"Time is returning," the voice said. "You are beginning to be aware of where you are." He could feel the metal plates against his leg. His hands were warm now. They were bathed in hot air that was slowly cooling. His neck tingled. He took a deep breath and felt his heart begin to speed up. Then he was fully conscious. The lights were gone. He was sitting in the dark room again, alone.

Immediately, the worries started. Did he do all right? What happened? He had faint memory of being on the moon, not much more. A residue of panic was nipping at a corner of his shoulder and his mind. He blinked a couple of times. Had he said the right things? Had he maintained his image?

"The test is now completed. Mr. Canyon, you were offered several options, and you chose the one appropriate for you. Each time you made a decision, you activated another series of options. That is why this test is unique to you. No one else will make the decision you selected. You will see the results reflected in your reading in a week." There was a click, and the voice stopped.

For a moment, Canyon wondered if he should leave. There had been no indication. Was this part of the test? Was the camera somewhere in the dark, shooting with an infrared lens? He tried to see, but there was only blackness. He looked down. There was no beacon to guide him. Finally, he stood up. He felt light-headed, wobbly.

A faint glow appeared by his foot. He turned to where the door should be. The light did not follow him. Bewildered he turned back. The path led in another direction. Again, he paused. He knew which way he had come, but could he find his way out without the light. Was this another test? He cursed the machinery that created all of this. He condemned the directors, the computers, the employees, everyone to hell for putting him in such a position. All silently, of course. His face never changed its placid expression. Finally, he turned and followed the light. He exited by a door underneath the color picture of the moon.

The waiting room was empty except for the clerk. Canyon looked over. The man glanced up and smiled. Then, slowly, he began to scowl. Ridges deepened in his forehead; his eyes narrowed.

Canyon smoothed his coat, stiffened his back, straightened his neck, flicked his sleeves and almost ran out of the room.

VIII

Fidgeting uneasily behind the row of screens, General Allistair McCaulley decided the time had come for an executive decision. He tucked in his shirt and buttoned his uniform coat which ballooned over his chest. He looked down at the expanse ruefully. Naturally, he had plenty of time to do something about that, but he would have to do *something*. He just wasn't sure what, particularly now that he had decided his next course of action. An aide brushed past him and hurried across the military control headquarters underground facility outside Washington, D.C. He didn't apologize, but McCaulley didn't mind. This was probably the only place he was not treated like some kind of idol. The men and women manning the screens, monitoring the various instruments and wandering like determined bees through the maze had better things to do than be awestruck with a fat general. His 3 rating meant little to most of them. He was a soldier and that was all. So McCaulley visited as often as possible.

As a sergeant—in what he laughingly called his previous incarnation—with minimal security clearance, he would not have been allowed in this secret headquarters. However, now that he was a 3, no door was shut. He pointed out that an enemy merely needed to get an infiltrator classified as a 3—admittedly a difficult task—to have complete access to all United States military secrets, but no one listened to that. McCaulley and his sense of humor, the president had sniffed. Besides, it may be all academic, now that the United Nations was again debating the elimination of the immortality drugs. Too many suicides, too much chaos. That sort of rubbish.

McCaulley had testified at the first two hearings on the topic and had helped defeat the initial proposal. However, some diehards had raised it again. Socialist nations were screaming their citizens were being shortchanged by the evaluation computers. They saw each negative vote as political. Third-world countries were chaffing for additional promotions, arguing their citizens needed some leaders to look up to. Others claimed money devoted to long-life research would be better invested in solving hunger, pollution, overpopulation and related problems. Such confusion, McCaulley sighed. But not in his mind, not when he had reached a conclusion.

He walked slowly through the crowded aisle. Majors and colonels were talking. No one saluted. Such formalities would have tied up manpower for hours. However, they quickly stepped aside for a rapidly moving captain. On the far wall, a giant map of the world was lit up with a variety of lights to indicate positions of certain planes, submarines and satellites. Officers were standing below it, pointing at something and asking for larger views.

"General?" someone said. McCaulley glanced up. He had been so preoccupied with finding his way through the crowd he hadn't noticed a lieutenant approach him. The officer held a piece of paper in her hand. "A communiqué." She held it out.

McCaulley licked his lips. "Young woman," he said, patting her arm, "there's something you should learn." He leaned over in a conspirator whisper. "When you see a general with an intense, determined look on his face, simply stand aside. There will be time for important messages when the real decisions have been reached."

"Yes, sir." However, she did not move aside so he could pass. "General Alsop requests an immediate response, sir."

McCaulley looked at her carefully. She was intently serious. "Lieutenant, how many stars does General Alsop have?" he finally asked.

"Two, sir."

"I have seven. Bear in mind, he would like five more. As a result, everything to him is important. To me, I already have seven so nothing is that important. Now, if you'd like, you can come with me. That way General Alsop will see you're not shirking your duty while," he patted his stomach, "I'm not shirking mine."

"Yes, sir." She dutifully fell in behind him. McCaulley took a deep breath and trudged on. If people only knew the hassle of being a 3, they would never strive so hard. There were always other generals demonstrating their status by sending him notes. Alsop may have been the worst. He was the one who signed the order sending McCaulley to the moon. Although he had reached a 2 himself, Alsop had apparently not gotten over the instant rise of his subordinate.

"If I had known what would happen on the Moon," he had grumbled once at a Pentagon party, "I would have sent a West Pointer."

Just think, McCaulley had told himself at the time, that little byplay could continue for another four centuries. It was enough to make any 3 turn in that little bottle of amber pills and bypass the endless rounds of medical checkups and, in McCaulley's case, medical lectures about diet and exercise. The general remembered his doctor's last words on that subject. He had ignored them. Golf was enough exercise for anyone. What did the doctor know about breaking 100! The damn physician was a scratch golfer, what with playing every Wednesday afternoon. McCaulley figured at the rate he was progressing, 100 should fall in maybe 50 years.

His immediate destination was finally in sight. He could see the small office on the far wall. The light was on, bright and inviting. That was what he had spotted from across the floor. There was something about that light that always drew him. He was sure it was the light. He was tempted to have it changed to something a bit more glaring. Maybe he would. Still, others might complain and there was no reason to start another controversy. Especially now. The president was upset about the Outsiders. Too many, he had insisted.

The Age Commission was listening, and everyone was thinking of ways to throw money at the problem. There were religious leaders to placate. They were harping "quality of life." A few holdouts were still bemoaning the drugs because they "interfered with God's order." McCaulley shook his head as all these thoughts cascaded through his tired brain. There wasn't a day some lobbyist on one side or another didn't corner him for a brief harangue.

Even his doctor had an opinion and had not hesitated to express it. "You carry weight," he noted, then eyed McCaulley's stomach. "Too much in some places."

"General," the lieutenant tried again.

"Aha," McCaulley wagged a finger at her.

"It really is important, sir."

She was so sincere. McCaulley glanced at her wistfully. He was that way once, too. He could hear the increase in conversations behind him, but he refused to stop, not this close to his quarry. "Will the world end in a few minutes?"

"I don't know, sir."

"Then the message will wait until you do." He stomped into the small room. She stood by the doorway. A delicious aroma floated up to him. The room was almost empty, but the four officers there were crowded around the table. Two were drinking coffee; two were listening. All four were bathed in that redolent scent. They moved aside for him. McCaulley ignored their glances. He had seen, and felt, them before. The delight at being picked out and identified had long since vanished.

There. He could see the tray. He sniffed deeply and enjoyed the view. There was nothing better than fresh donuts. That had been his first contribution to the underground facility. When he arrived, there was only coffee. It took him only a moment to discover the absence of his favorite food and demand immediate corrective action. Now they were accepted as standard fare. That's the way traditions started.

McCaulley surveyed the options. Powdered donuts were nice, but there was no reason to dust his uniform. His wife, now sadly departed, always chastised him for not thinking of such things. The jelly ones were also delicious, but not his favorites. He recalled one embarrassing meeting with the president only to be told an hour later about the cherry smear over his lips. Finally, he took the cream-filled, chocolate-covered éclair. A 7-star general should not be seen wavering over pastry. A quick decision, a fast hand. Like poker. Only at this, he didn't lose.

He bit quickly and stuffed the remainder into his mouth. Training showed every time, and McCaulley had trained both his mouth and appetite to accommodate everything his mind decided upon. He took a second donut and, still chewing, started for the door. He was enjoying the taste of the first and savoring the thought of the second when he ran into the lieutenant again. She had been patiently waiting for him to finish.

"The note, sir," she said. There was a hint of exasperation in her voice.

McCaulley took it with his free hand. He didn't carry a cellphone, so a written message was the only way to reach him. Slowly, as he munched his donut, he read. It was a request for him to come immediately to the conference room. Urgent, the memo said. He swallowed the remains of the first donut and started on the second, rereading as he devoured. Alsop was not given to panic or alarms despite his tendency to write too many notes. On the other hand, he would not ask for McCaulley to come for a conference unless there was something of major importance. The general didn't have much faith in McCaulley's training or intelligence, a fact he demonstrated at every opportunity.

The lieutenant obviously wanted an answer. He handed her the note, wiped his face with a napkin and gave her that, too. "Tell him I will be there as soon as possible." She started away. "Oh," he called after her, "tell him you couldn't find me at first. Tell him I was in a top-level security briefing."

She saluted with a smile, turned and hurried away. McCaulley wondered if he should get another donut. No, he told himself, he would just enjoy Alsop's disgust when he arrived. There were no calories in that.

He started to walk back and suddenly realized he did not know which conference room Alsop was in. Maybe it was in the note. He couldn't remember. Damn. Alsop would give him one of those evil glares when he did manage to arrive. He probably should get that donut. Instead, he forced himself to walk along the outer ridge. Which room was Alsop likely to use? What a very annoying bother.

He grabbed the first lieutenant he could find and drew the young man aside. The officer's eyes grew wide at this sudden interruption in routine. "Soldier," McCaulley said firmly, glancing around him as if not wanting anyone to overhear, "what I tell you must be kept top secret." The lieutenant nodded. McCaulley rubbed his chin. Another West Pointer. Clean-cut, trim, athletic. It was disgusting. "General Alsop and I are involved in a private conference. We are communicating only with code to avoid detection. We think there may be a traitor in our midst." The lieutenant paled. "Now, to avoid detection, we have arranged a way to meet so we both know the coast is clear. For that, I need you."

"Yes, sir." The officer gulped.

McCaulley leaned over closely. "You are to go to the conference room where General Alsop is, open the door and say, 'The fig tree is loose.'"

"The fig tree is loose."

"Exactly." He took the lieutenant's sleeve and almost leaned on his chest. "If General Alsop looks up and doesn't say anything, the coast is clear."

"Yes, sir."

"Can you do it?"

"Yes, sir."

"Alright, now walk slowly and look as though nothing is happening." McCaulley released the sleeve, and the officer moved hesitantly away.

He suddenly stopped. "Which conference room?" he whispered.

"Aha," McCaulley said firmly. "We have to keep some things secret or…" he wagged a finger.

"Yes, sir," the lieutenant nodded. He began to walk with a very determined march, weaving in and out of the throng, his shoulders thrown back. Humming to himself, McCaulley followed behind. The lieutenant turned down the first corridor and tried all four doors. No Alsop. The same was true for the next three corridors, which extended like spokes away from the central hall. McCaulley was beginning to think he had been too clever when the lieutenant strode up the fifth corridor. The officer was not the least bit tired by his exercise, but the general was puffing and falling farther behind with each passing step. He was also getting envious of the way the young man opened each door with a firm, sudden twist of his wrist. Those doors were heavy.

The first door was enough. The lieutenant boomed out, "The fig tree is loose," waited and then waved to McCaulley. "All clear, sir."

"Quiet," the general gasped as he finally drew alongside.

"Yes, sir."

"Not a word to anyone," he continued in an undertone.

"Yes, sir." The lieutenant winked and left. McCaulley gaped. Maybe he had used that ploy too often. Stories do get around even though he told participants to keep quiet. Maybe he should threaten a court martial or something drastic. That would stop them from gossiping.

He stepped inside. The door thudded behind him. Alsop was bent over an electronic map. There was a projection of terrain on the screen. The general glanced over at McCaulley and sighed. "We obviously have different definitions of immediately," he said. "The fig tree is loose?" There was no one else in the room. McCaulley knew Alsop would not be so brusque if anyone else were present. If nothing else, Alsop understood military courtesy in public.

"You got me at a bad time."

"Apparently," Alsop sniffed. "You still have cream on your cheek." He went back to examining the map. "Come here and look at this." McCaulley wiped the residue with a handkerchief and hurried over. Alsop pointed a bony finger at a point on the map. "Heard the report?" He didn't wait for a reply. "It landed about here." He gestured up at the screen. There was a corresponding blinking red light in the center of the map displayed there.

"When?" McCaulley asked. He was going to say "what" but decided to display his ignorance later in the conversation. That must be what all the buzzing was about on the floor.

"In the last fifteen minutes."

"What are signals picking up?" This was serious. McCaulley erased the smile from his mouth and the memory of his brief repast from his mind. Anything landing on American territory was serious.

"NORAD just pinpointed a blip on the screen; that's all." Alsop continued to survey the map. He was a tall, thin man with concave cheeks that seemed to be sucked back into his face. Like many on the 2 level, he had been promoted after his hair had begun to pick up a gray tinge, and deep lines had sprouted on his face. He would look that way 200 years from now, McCaulley thought. He shivered slightly at that idea. The man resembled a ghost now. And as humorless as one. Alsop thought of nothing but logistics and supplies. He was incredibly good at those functions; that's how he won his rating. Still, McCaulley reasoned, a person devoted to such dried up statistics was bound to end up looking like a withered computer printout. General Alsop came as close as any human could.

McCaulley leaned over the map. The area looked familiar. "Any other data?"

"NORAD lost it over Utah. Radar traced it to Arizona. It was taking evasive action." Alsop stared at McCaulley. "I can get fifteen hundred men there in two hours, with support about four hundred miles away, at least eight tanks. It can be surrounded."

"It could be a damn glider," McCaulley countered. That had happened before. Alsop had talked him into a full-scale alert for a glider that had drifted off course. Explaining that one was hard, particularly with that many troops standing around with their automatic lasers pointed at a poor, frightened pilot.

"Negative," Alsop said. He hadn't been the least bit perturbed by the incident. The men were better off there than sitting in their barracks. Besides, he insisted, the march did them good. McCaulley had visions of a permanently marching mass of soldiers, being wheeled around the United States like pawns on a chess board. Rigid and firm, Alsop had not bowed to any criticism. McCaulley, on the other hand, had eaten far beyond his doctor's suggested diet in frustration. Of course, he had freely admitted, he would have eaten more in celebration if that had been warranted.

"It's a metallic object that entered the earth's atmosphere. I do not believe the Chinese are capable of such a maneuver, although," Alsop scratched his chin, "this could be a test." He considered that.

"I have asked the President to contact the Chinese Premier."

McCaulley cocked an eyebrow at him. "We do move fast."

"One of us should," Alsop replied acidly. He jabbed a finger on a spot. "Why land right in the middle of the desert?" He ran that concept through his mind. McCaulley could almost see it being shifted from level to level, cascading downward like beach sand roughed up by the tide and spewing into the ocean. "I felt some action was necessary."

"Of course you did." McCaulley soothed. Being second in command was not an easy life for a duty-bound officer, particularly when the superior had such few military talents. "I can understand your thinking. And be assured, I will include your prompt action of going over my head in my report." Alsop visibly tightened, but did not reply. "Now, you were saying about the actual landing site?"

"Desert. It's about one hundred fifty miles southeast of Phoenix, near the Mexican border. The Colorado dries up within a few miles. Nothing but some scraggly plants, mesquite, cactus, that sort of thing." Alsop reported. His tone changed.

McCaulley studied the terrain. The large map showed the topographical features. Nothing appeared threatened. There were no military facilities nearby. Still, someone could be attempting to drop agents. Or just running an experiment. Or creating a ruse to redirect attention. Everything had to be considered. The ideas didn't float as easily through his brain; they tended to clog every few seconds. It was his decision, however. As supreme commander, any moves were his responsibility. He took a deep breath and patted his ample belly. That always seemed to relax him. He could almost hear Alsop begin to crackle with impatience. The general was so brittle and withered, McCaulley was convinced one day Alsop would just crumple into little gray bits of parchment and float through the air like ash from a dying fire.

"I don't like this at all," McCaulley temporized.

"I want to send troops in," Alsop said immediately. "I think we should surround it. Who knows what might be getting out right now?"

"What did you have in mind?"

"Maybe they're testing a gas. Germ warfare. Anything."

"And you want fifteen hundred men walking into that?"

Alsop hesitated. "I have gas masks in their supplies. And antidotes. They'll be properly prepared."

McCaulley smiled. "One of us should be," he said in his calm, relaxed voice.

"We are," Alsop continued icily. Then, both returned to their map reading.

"Any reports from the flybys?" McCaulley finally asked.

"Not yet."

"Then let's wait for them. It could be a satellite that left orbit."

Alsop shook his head. "We'd have a report."

McCaulley shrugged. "And is the equipment always perfect? We can wait a few more minutes." They did. Alsop studied the map as though his eyes could somehow read an answer in the light coloring of southeastern Arizona. McCaulley, in contrast, finally sat down. One thing was sure; he wasn't going to see for himself. One visit to that territory was enough. Lord knows, he might have to deal with that character from Phoenix. That man was crazy, and he wasn't going to risk exposure a second time. He thought back and chuckled.

Alsop glanced at him. "Thinking of supper?" he asked. "Or an amusing breakfast?"

"Both." McCaulley hid a sigh. It wasn't easy leading a man like this. Yet, Alsop knew what he was doing. That was the only compensation.

There was a slight ping from the computer. Alsop pressed a control on the side of the screen. Images immediately popped up. McCaulley could not see them from his position and reluctantly stood. He had hoped for a few more minutes to collect his thoughts and to let the donuts settle in his stomach.

Alsop gasped slightly. He tapped the central object in the clear HD image. "Now what?" he asked. His voice was low and harsh.

McCaulley swallowed hard. The picture soured the brief bits of donuts still in his mouth. On the middle of the picture was a ship. It looked to be golden colored. It was sitting upright and pointing toward the sky. There was an odd-shaped insignia toward the base, something like a distorted Y. He ran through the electronic images one after the other. They were of the same ship from different angles. There was no sign of life.

"We may need your troops," he finally said. "Alsop, see if intelligence has something on that symbol. I don't want to find we've surrounded a public relations masterpiece from a smart corporation."

"Yes, sir."

McCaulley sighed. He had never gotten used to the saluting and other formalities. One minute, he's a noncom on the moon, the next he is being rapidly promoted with stars replacing his stripes. At one point, he wondered if his sloping shoulders would be large enough for the seven stars. He had visions of them extending down his sleeve the way a long name on an athlete's jersey is stretched around the back. The parades. The speeches. Every now and then, he would wake up and think he was still being feted somewhere. That's where all of this excess weight came from. He was thin once. And taller. And there was Alsop, lean as a side of artificial bacon, waiting eagerly to get going.

McCaulley could understand the enthusiasm. He saw it in the eyes of so many. A chance. That's all they wanted. The same fluke chance to receive an instant pass to the 3 level. Anything might happen in an assignment. Who knew what would occur on a dull, boring stay on the Moon? Perhaps the same thing might happen in the desert, or on the mountains. Alsop's chin was trembling with impatience. McCaulley almost looked away to avoid making a comment about it. Here was a general who probably needed charcoal under his bed to warm the frozen gel in his blood, and he was so excited about an opportunity to put something stimulating on the computer he could barely stand there.

"I think you'd better get the men in motion before you go," McCaulley said.

Alsop nodded. "I took the liberty of issuing that order when the first reports arrived." He began to collect the photos. "Knowing your reputation for quick, decisive action, I realized you would be disappointed if your subordinates failed to emulate."

"Is that rehearsed?"

Alsop cleared his throat. His tone was hard and swift. "I have already had the immediate areas cleared of civilians," he reported.

McCaulley was not impressed. "Jackrabbits, too? There is no one within one hundred miles of that landing site."

"Outsiders are near there," Alsop said. "But I'll take care of the rabbits. I knew you'd be a stickler for such details." He put the photos in the envelope. "Military personnel from Phoenix will arrive shortly before we do and secure the camp site. The men had been ordered from Tucson Airport. They will arrive in," he checked his watch, "forty two minutes. In addition, all surveillance will continue."

"Who is in charge there?"

Alsop did not even consult his notes. "A Walter Canyon. Colonel Seavers, who was regional officer, has been transferred and no replacement has been named."

There was no inflection, but McCaulley wondered. Alsop knew about the turkey massacre. He couldn't have missed either the news reports or the discussion, and he certainly didn't miss McCaulley's joke in the debriefing session just a week ago. He had laughed. Still, it would not be above him to name Canyon, to pinpoint him, just to irritate McCaulley. He stared into Alsop's pale blue eyes, but could find no hint of emotion. "Will that be all, sir?" Alsop asked briskly.

McCaulley was beginning to regret sending Alsop to Arizona, but there was no one else who could grasp the situation as quickly or as completely. He was bound to overreact, but that could be handled. "No fireworks," McCaulley wagged a finger. He put it down as soon as he spotted telltale cream clinging to a nail. "I want this one quiet. No media, nothing."

"Yes, sir."

"For a change, if this turns out to be another of your false alarms, let's get out of it with nothing more than a few embarrassed explanations to the President. I'm tired of getting egg on my face." McCaulley said firmly.

"I certainly understand that," Alsop murmured. He saluted and was gone before McCaulley realized what he had said. He looked around in frustration. Just his image off the paneled walls looked back. For a moment, he hesitated to leave. He was not used to quiet. In here, no one could hear him, look at him, or talk to him. That was some consolation for McCaulley. Still, he couldn't stay here forever. He was due at the White House to brief the President. By the time he arrived, Alsop should have handled this crisis with ease.

Reluctantly, he walked to the door. His heavy tread was swallowed up immediately by the sound-proof floors and ceiling.

McCaulley looked around one last time before leaving. He would need fortification for any more meetings that were sure to follow. And he knew just where he was going to get it. That was reason enough to close the door and exit. Exercise? He snapped at the imaginary doctor as he hurried along. What do you call this?

IX

Something broke the eerie silence with a sudden move. Walter Canyon held his breath before he spotted a lizard racing across the hot sand to get out of the sun. It disappeared into the shade of some nearby rocks. He watched it with disgust. What was this world coming to? That lizard was more comfortable than he was. Sweat was running down his legs. His shirt was soaked. He would have left his suit coat on an obliging cactus if he hadn't thought the idea of approaching an alien ship without it would have made him look ridiculous. How much time did he have? He checked his watch. Just 30 minutes. Then Alsop would be here, and this little trip would be discovered. Not much time, but enough, if all went well, to merit a promotion.

He had to do something to counter his steadily declining ratings. A solo mission to confront an alien seemed the ideal way to reverse the ratings plunge.

Grimly, Canyon walked on. He could see the large golden hull of the alien craft in front of him. It hadn't moved, but he didn't feel any closer to it.

Just 15 minutes ago, he had left the horde of newsmen who had descended on their base camp and started on this trek. No media, McCaulley had ordered and Alsop had demanded. The command came far too late. The ship had already been photographed, and its image was flashing through innumerable communication devises worldwide.

The military commander, Col. Beck, had been livid. Canyon simply added to his outrage. A small, thin man with a bald head and glasses, Beck had almost jumped up and down to protest Canyon's intended personal excursion to the ship. "This is a military matter," he kept saying.

Canyon had looked as haughty as possible, staring down at the miniature officer. He knew what Beck wanted. The colonel couldn't disguise it, despite his anger. Beck wanted to be the one seen with the alien. Beck wanted to be in the pictures, in the papers, on television, on computer tape as the one who had captured the alien, who made first contact. Anyone could see that. Beck's eyes bulged; his lips quivered in fury, but Canyon was not moved. Gen. Alsop had placed him in charge, and he had made his decision. The history books would read that Walter Marson Canyon had made the first contact with an alien being.

Triumphantly, he had ordered the troops to stay no closer than half a mile from the alien vessel. Then he had started out, cursing the dry, encrusted soil every step of the way. His feet were sore and his eyes hurt, but he could not stop. People would understand, he told himself as he licked his dry lips. What choice did I have? His ratings were down dramatically. He had failed his evaluation. His assistants were consistently outshining him. Sinone was already being mentioned for an opening in another district that was twice as important. Cataline was considered the bright new star in the headquarters' staff. The arrival of an alien craft was like manna.

There was a shadow from a cloud overhead that startled him. Canyon hesitated again. He felt the gun at his waist. It was nestled comfortably inside his suit coat. The quartermaster had been reluctant to issue it, but Canyon had ordered him to comply. Then he threw in a lie that he was certified. Maybe that was designed to ease both of their conscience. Canyon rubbed the hard metal and then took his hand away. He didn't want to fire it accidently. That would undermine his image.

The ground crunched underfoot. It seemed so loud in this quiet world. He looked to the left and could see the shadows of men guarding that side. More men to the other side. As soon as Alsop came, they would close in and shut him out. They were just waiting. One of them might just find a way to intrude, to earn some notoriety. That would be awful. Canyon trudged on.

The ship intrigued him. It was long with manta-like wings on both sides. It was resting on a slight angle, balanced on a device connected near the base. He had run over various options in his mind. He could stand outside and shout, although that seemed tinged with ridiculousness. What would the alien think, hearing strange, belligerent words?

He thought about marching up to the front—or wherever the door was—spreading his legs gunfighter style and just waiting. No one could mistake that challenge. That approach had both the advantage of simplicity and the ease of motion. He really wouldn't have to do anything but stand. He considered it. The picture appeared in his mind—strong, brave, forceful Walter Canyon. Just the thing for popular consumption. He forced a smile. That cracked his lower lip and reminded him he should have prepared a little better for the hike. But there had been no time to gather water. Alsop was coming; his own opportunity was slipping away at the same pace.

He was near enough now to the ship to be impressed by the height. It towered above him. There were no obvious rivets or seams. The craft seemed to have been built in a single unit. There were no signs of weaponry, no hint of danger. He wondered if the area around the ship was mined in some way. Perhaps everyone inside was dead. Anything was possible. Then what would he do? He would look foolish standing here while the troops came up. What if the aliens attacked? McCaulley held his own, Canyon told himself, he could, too. He curled his hand around the gun and pulled it out.

He had no idea how to use it.

Just pull the trigger, the sergeant had said. She was the only one who knew about Canyon's ignorance. But, Canyon thought, that knowledge won't do her much good where she was going to be transferred to.

He was near the tail now. He could see evidence of damage: a thick dent; charred metal. The engines seemed tiny from this vantage point, certainly much too small for interspace travel. No huge boosters. No second and third stages. The aliens must have another form of propulsion. Canyon smiled. He liked that image, too: Walter Marson Canyon, the father of modern space travel, the man who wrung the secrets from aliens and made modern planet hopping possible.

He moved around slowly. The afternoon was quiet. Somewhere overhead, sleek satellites were filming everything. And somewhere, Canyon knew, Gen. Alsop was viewing this scene, impotently murmuring to himself. There was nothing he could do, nothing anyone could do. Canyon was in control here. He circled the ship once without finding any doors. Puzzled, he stood back. Suddenly, he heard a snap, as if something had broken. He started to run toward the noise on the other side of the ship and then composed himself. A commander did not run. So, he strode.

A small glass-like bubble was standing open on the ground. There were two creatures standing beside it. Canyon did not react at first. He simply stopped and looked. One was a small, plastic-like horse; the other a yellow-skin being with light blonde hair, slits for eyes, virtually no nose and no ears. His lips were vertical rather than horizontal.

"Hello," the being said casually.

That did it. Canyon gaped. "Halt," he cried hoarsely from his rehearsed repertoire. He had expected to shout dramatically and force the aliens to stand still. Instead, one of them was starting up a conversation. He held the gun at them, but the effect was ruined by his nerves. He kept jerking the gun around like the tail of a cat.

"Ah," Anton said. "Like Hamlet's father." He searched his memory. Those months learning the language with Thurgose were obviously important. "My hour is almost come," he intoned. "When I to sulfurous and tormenting flames must render up myself."

Canyon lowered the gun. What was going on? "What?" he asked. The damn thing was speaking English. Was this a trick? Had Sinone set this up? No, that was not possible.

Anton shook his head. "Wrong line," he corrected. "You're supposed to say 'Alas, poor ghost.'"

"Ghost?" Canyon began to feel awful. The sun was getting to him. He should have worn a hat. The doctor had warned him. He should have listened. He could feel it pounding at him.

~ * ~

Anton considered the problem. Perhaps he had the wrong plan. This native was clearly confused. "Hmm, Banquo's ghost?" he thought aloud. Another possibility. Of course, the "halt" was not appropriate. "Thou canst not say I did it. Never shake thy gory locks at me," he offered. No, that was not it. Maybe the whole idea of ghosts was wrong. This native might have been affected by the ship or something. What other possibilities were there?

He tried Mark Twain's biography, a brief story of how Twain, as a young man, pretended to be hypnotized. He told the story briefly. Again, the native did not respond, but simply gaped. Perhaps a little more confusion. It was hard to tell. The native was sweating. Perspiration rolled down his face. His eyes seemed pale; his manner odd. He could barely stand still. Anton glanced at Thurgose. The little horse was light green. It was aiming its nose gun at the native just in case.

Maybe something a bit more modern. "Marley's ghost," Anton offered. His mind was flooded with other references. "Ho, ho, ho on a dead man's chest. Fifteen men and a bottle of rum." Nothing. "I'm the crew and the captain bold and the mate of the Nancy Brig." Still no sign of recognition. "Like a bridge over troubled waters," Anton sang. "I will lay me down." The native's gun was now dangling at the side. Anton wondered if that could be taken as an indication. "I can't get no satisfaction," he continued. "I try and I try and I try." The native's lips were moving but no words came out.

Anton wondered now at the odd clothes. He could see the man's feet weren't bare. He was getting used to that disappointment. His were, but the native had on heavy leather shoes. And a thick, black, cloth coat and pants. Maybe that was the official outfit. For a moment, Anton wished he had worn his ritualistic suit, but dropped that thought. Let the native face him as he was: tunic and pants. He did not need any artificial aids. Of course, he had fashioned a skyla stick from what had been a small toy. It wasn't much, but it felt good under his tunic, next to his skin. Discouraged, but not willing to give up, he plunged on. "Don't cry for me Argentina. The truth is I never left you." No reaction. "Memories. Alone in the moonlight." Nothing.

Anton stared at Thurgose. "I thought you taught me things people recognized."

"Perhaps you are still inhabiting the wrong century." Thurgose replied. He, too, spoke English. They had agreed to that as a learning device.

Anton nodded. "The winter chill of lasting ice settled over New England," he recited. Nothing. "There," he told Thurgose. "As modern as possible. I just learned that yesterday."

"Do not desist. We should make some method of contact."

"All right," Anton muttered. "Where helping hands do bequeath the sighs of man locked beneath a mournful eye. And time moves not at all like a ship on a doldrum sea or a drunk, against a wall, eyes open, breathing heavily." He had stressed each word in hopes of activating some gesture, some sign of recognition. The native did not do anything, but sway uneasily and turn even paler than before. Anton thought that might be the indication he was looking for, but decided no, the native would say something.

Swaying like a small, stiff tree, Canyon just toppled over in a dead faint.

Thurgose moved closer to study the situation closer. "I believe," it said cautiously, "that you have succeeded in overwhelming him with words."

"These people are very sensitive," Anton noted. He wanted to study the native at close range, but hesitated until Thurgose had completed the examination. The little horse was changing colors rapidly as it evaluated every possibility. It picked up the native's gun in its mouth and flung it away. "Primitive," it sniffed.

Anton waited quietly. He could hear the roar of planes far overhead. At the same time, there was a nice sense of quiet. The air was peaceful here. A bit cool, perhaps, but peaceful. Colors were muted, however. None of the bright hues of home, but scraggly greens and yellows, a few browns and blacks. Not much else. This was a disappointing planet. The males did not bare their feet to the elements. They didn't choose bright colors to flaunt their strength. They were pretty odd looking, too. Still, they had potential. They might just be of some assistance. There was obviously no way he could merge easily into their society. His appearance was just too different. However, they might help him return home and rebuild Dalia.

That thought had dominated his last few months.

Natives couldn't be that bad. After all, they had sent one person, barely armed to greet him. And they were susceptible to words. He just wished he knew which words had overwhelmed this person. Probably different people were affected by different words. Thurgose had not picked up that idiosyncrasy during earlier probes. However, it was nice to know now. Until the native awoke, he would wait.

Anton plopped down on the cool surface and looked around. Just one sun here. It would be easier to work out times of day. Too bad the place was so cold, however. No wonder the natives wore such thick clothing.

There was a sudden clap as a jet broke the sound barrier nearby. For a moment, Anton wondered if Wyron had come. That thought had plagued him from the moment they had left Quito. It had clung to the back of his mind, burning like a hot brick, until he almost shouted in anger. At some place, some time, he would face that Kajan and end the torment. Maybe the people here could aid in that, too. There was always a chance.

~ * ~

Meanwhile, in a plane now over Kansas, Gen. Alsop grimly surveyed the television screen. He could see Canyon clearly stretched out on the ground. The director had been standing one minute and then collapsed the next. No alien weapons were visible. Perhaps they used magnetic forces. Who knew what these aliens were capable of?

He stared down at his arithmetic. On a piece of paper, he had sketched out troop movements and supplies. More than 2,000 men were now on their way to reinforce troops on the ground. In addition, tanks, laser-firing armored rollers, mortars and other equipment was being rolled into place. Alsop was ready. He would capture those aliens. McCaulley would get no credit for this. The fat commander was safely behind the lines. This was Alsop's show. "Can't this jet go any faster?" he snarled at an aide.

"No, sir," the captain stammered.

"That wasn't a question, captain," Alsop continued. "That was an order."

"Yes, sir." The aide vanished into the cockpit.

Alsop didn't watch him go. His mind was rapidly weighing all of the options. They would have to find what the alien wanted, what sort of weaponry he had, what they could learn from him, how dangerous he was. He wrote all of his ideas down. The notes would join the hundreds of others he produced every day. They would all go into his book someday. He began to write. Anything to avoid looking out the windows. General Alsop was afraid of heights.

In Washington, Gen. McCaulley paced his small office. Newsmen were gathered in the press room waiting for words from him and the president. The president had just gotten a complete briefing. No, McCaulley didn't know what was going on with Canyon. Yes, he might be dead. Yes, they may have to attack the aliens if they turn out to be violent. Yes, Canyon's jackass action was going to jeopardize the United Nations' hearings. Some delegates were already pointing out what happened when a 3 rating was dangled in front of a would-be hero's eyes. Canyon had grabbed at it, and, in the process, might have jeopardized the first concrete meeting with an alien.

Delegates were furious with the United States for entrusting such a delicate mission to a local director. At the same time, everyone seemed to realize it didn't matter who was there, someone would have tried for a similar move to achieve a higher rating. Proof, several delegates insisted, that the idea of ratings were more damaging than helpful.

Not so, McCaulley had protested through an assistant. Canyon was demonstrating the personal courage motivated by the high rating. He had made contact. If he surrendered his life, perhaps it will help save others. Not too many were impressed. McCaulley could feel the tide turning. He would have to testify himself and let Alsop handle the alien for the moment. "Damn," he muttered. All this did was activate his appetite. He needed quiet if he were going to diet. There was a knock on the door.

"Yes."

"The media is ready," a familiar voice said.

McCaulley opened the door carefully. His aide was there. Behind him, there were hundreds of reporters. He checked his cellphone one more time and then headed to the podium. He could see the eager faces, the question already bursting in air. Lights blared. The small computer tablet on the dais beeped. Alsop had landed near the alien craft.

McCaulley turned off his phone and stood behind the podium. The throng buzzed as he waited for silence. Behind him, the image of the alien ship loomed on a screen. McCaulley glanced up at the image: Canyon, the alien and the small animal that rolled around were gone. McCaulley's mouth dropped.

"The general will now take questions," the aide intoned, prompting a thicket of hands to shoot into the air.

~ * ~

"They took him inside," an aide informed Alsop in Arizona as he stepped down from the plane. A mass of local reporters were being kept to one side of the airplane. They were shouting questions at him through armed military police who had formed a human barricade.

"When?"

"Seconds ago."

"How?" Alsop picked up his pace. The limousine was waiting. They were a mile from the camp, and the car was the fastest way to the site. The helicopter had been used to shuttle a presidential assistant. Alsop always had a backup. He climbed inside; the aide followed. In here, at least, there was quiet. And, to Alsop's delight, the vehicle stayed on the ground.

"The trained pony seemed to have some kind of carrying unit on its back. It scooped up Canyon and carried him inside. The alien followed. He must be the trainer or something. That's one smart horse," the aide reported.

Alsop glared. "Don't tell me what you think." He paused to consider the new information. "Have they started their engines?"

"No, sir."

Alsop switched on the car's television set. He could see the ship clearly now. The aide slid a tablet in front of him filled with information on the location of fighter planes and support troops. Alsop did not show any emotion, but he could see that the ship would never take off. At least 15 jets were ready with heat-seeking missiles. Unless the alien vessel was made of material capable of withstanding a tremendous assault, it would never leave Earth.

He texted that information to McCaulley, writing quickly in military jargon no one else could possibly understand. Then he sat there quietly, watching the scenery speed by, listening to the sirens and thinking.

~ * ~

Inside the ship, Canyon was beginning to stir. He propped himself up on his elbows and looked around with bleary eyes. The ship was very warm, but at least the sun wasn't beating down on him. He could see the bright colors; they practically jumped off the wall at him. And the spectacular ceiling. It was ablaze in red, blue and gold. His mind cleared, and he could focus again. The alien was looking at him. Canyon's first reaction was to gasp, then reach in his pocket for a gun. It wasn't there. Almost instantly, the horse slid between him and the alien. They stared at him together.

"Hello," the alien said. "I don't know what words hurt you, but if you'll tell me, I won't use them again."

He had a pleasant voice. There was a strong accent, but Canyon could understand what the alien said. He just couldn't understand why he understood it. "You speak English," Canyon finally replied.

The alien seemed to brighten. He patted the horse. "Thurgose," he exclaimed, "you did it." He nodded at Canyon. "To be recognized for your effort is higher praise than applause and almost as good as being kissed on the cheek by your mother. Lysanda, about twelve hundred," he said.

Thurgose shook his head. "Try anew."

"About eleven hundred," the alien offered.

"Anew," the horse said firmly. Canyon watched this byplay with open-eyed amazement. Clearly, the alien reported to the horse. This was becoming too much for him again. He groaned and lay back.

"Maybe he's got more than one dangerous word?" Anton said.

"It was nine hundred," Thurgose instructed firmly. "You were considering Lycastra who lived in the twelve hundreds." It turned and pointed an ear at Anton. "I conceived we had neglected your studies much too long. You have omitted to recall the significant details. What would your father say me if he had overheard your failure? I am abashed by your performance for it signifies I have been most derelict."

Canyon licked his lips. "Excuse me," he tried.

Thurgose was not through. "I will have to write a reprimand in the daily log book and find suitable deleterious markings to compensate for such a failing."

Anton ran a hand along the horse's stomach. "I was afraid of this," he said sadly. He pressed a button, and a small door slid open in Thurgose's left hip. The horse rambled on until Anton found one of the small circuit breakers. The horse stopped in mid-sentence.

"It has been so tired lately," Anton continued as he rolled Thurgose back toward the grooves near the energy supply. "All that checking and rechecking. I told it to eat, but you know how guardians can be." He guided Thurgose into place. Almost immediately, the little horse turned pink. Anton rubbed his hand along its special sensitive area on the scalp. Thurgose sighed. As if remembering Canyon, Anton suddenly turned and bounded cheerily across the room. "Now you, too."

Canyon shrank away. "What do you want with me?" He tried to disguise the tremor in his voice, but couldn't. All the marvelous images of heroism and valor just faded away. Instead, he had a dark picture of being transported millions of light years away where ratings meant nothing and all of his efforts to reach level 2 would be futile.

Anton plopped down beside him. "I need help," he said.

"Help?" That wasn't the answer Canyon expected.

"I need help rebuilding my planet."

Canyon shuddered. "I really don't know anything about construction." He stopped. "You came here for a few carpenters?" He felt some strength coming back so he stood up and stretched his back. His shoulder hurt.

"I guess." Anton didn't recognize the word. This native certainly didn't seem interested, however. That was disappointing. He could just imagine hordes of eager explorers ready to join him in his expedition. They could find another planet where he could be their Frighem. He was offering them a new land, plenty of fresh air, delicacies they could just begin to conceive of, not to mention their own Frighem to rule over them. Maybe that was the problem. They might have their own monarch who would object to his subjects simply flying away. That would be easy to solve. He'd create a liaison with the ruler's daughter however distasteful she might look. Symbolism, his father had insisted, is everything. Thurgose had told him about the possibility of other monarchs. Growing up on Dalia with its one-family rule, Anton hadn't considered that likelihood before.

"Brubiscon," Thurgose had cautioned him, "Never assume you are alone, regardless of your station." That point might be worth considering at this stage.

"Who is your Frighem?" Anton tried eagerly.

Canyon stiffened. Finally, he was ready. "I represent the United States of America. On behalf of the President and the Congress of these United States, I welcome you to the planet Earth." He then introduced himself as the selected delegate. Anton, who had heard many speeches in his time, lost his attention very quickly as Canyon moved on to a description of "these United States" and an explanation of the United Nations, the divide between capitalism and socialism, and the rest. He finished without a smile. Anton studied his own feet.

Canyon looked down and saw the sores. "We also have excellent medical facilities here." He pointed at Anton's feet. "We'll heal those."

Paling rapidly, Anton pulled his feet back. He almost blurted something in Dalian, but caught himself. This representative was no better than the most backward of his subjects. Heal the scars of manhood? What an insult. He felt his skla stick and considered bringing it out. Behind him, Thurgose clucked. That was enough. Anton calmed down.

He then launched into his own description of both his status and of Dalia, puffing himself up with each title until he was as tall as he could be. He was still much shorter than Canyon, but he felt taller. He could see Canyon's eyes widen as the list went on.

~ * ~

"What are they doing in there?" an aide asked Alsop as the general stared at the ship. He did not pace. That would reveal nerves. He stood, hands behind him, and stared as if he could see through the metal sheath that surrounded the craft.

Alsop did not answer the question. "Has the report gone to the reporters?" he snapped instead.

"Yes, sir."

Alsop nodded. That might cool things off. Another glider had been found; that's what the reporters would be told. The pilot was to be released shortly. That pilot—selected from the General's own aides—would carefully lie to prevent further interest. Someday, the truth might leak out, but not before the alien had been squeezed of all information. This was no time for a media convention. This was too important.

~ * ~

In Washington, McCaulley was chatting with reporters at a press conference and lying. He was following the same line. As he spoke, he studied faces to see what impact his words were having. He saw reporters he had known for 40 years—all now gray and tired look-ing—watching back. He could almost read what was really going through their minds: how young he looked; how old they were. That was a thought he saw in everyone's eyes. Sometimes, it even haunted him. With a tinge of sadness in his voice, he answered their questions and fabricated everything. This time, however, he would not take the blame for this. He directed all the criticism at General Alsop. If nothing else, it felt good as he heaped the insults on with the same hefty measure he used to add sugar to his coffee.

~ * ~

Inside the ship, Canyon was trying to explain what Anton would be asked to do. Media was a new idea to the alien. His family con-trolled all communication. Television was completely unknown, alt-hough radio was commonplace. Computers had eliminated the need for visual contact with almost instantaneous exchanges. The free press concept was even more foreign. However, he liked the idea of a news conference. A simple invitation could reach millions of peo-ple. There was only one concern: what if he selected the words that caused people everywhere to collapse?

"One thing," he said to Canyon. "I don't want to offend any-one. Are there words I shouldn't use so no one will get hurt?"

"Hurt?"

"Like I hurt you," Anton explained. "You fell over."

Canyon stepped back and stiffened his neck. "I did no such

thing. I used a ruse to lure my way inside. It was carefully planned."

"I didn't know." Anton apologized.

Canyon was not ready to let that go. "You will not tell anyone what happened. I will explain. This is a matter of grave importance, and you will not say something wrong." Anton began to wish Canyon had a small power source that could be shut off.

Thurgose whispered something and Anton stepped back to hear. "Logic," he was repeating.

Anton nodded. "To know the heart of man," he recited, "merely raise a single failing. Hurcos 1512."

"Very good," Thurgose said weakly.

"I hope that's clear," Canyon finished. He glared at his prisoners. None of this had gone as he had expected, but, at the same time, he would usher them into the world. He feverishly conjured up visions of parades and speeches. No more planning. He would be the one in the center, waving to the crowd. And he would be the one who enjoyed carte blanche. McCaulley? That fat general would hold him up, not the other way around. And he'd tell jokes about McCaulley's appetite and ban any comments about turkeys. That made him feel better. "It is time to go," he said firmly.

Anton glanced at Thurgose. The little horse nodded. Anton reattached the motor drive, and Thurgose rolled away from the grooves. Almost immediately, it turned a protective green shade.

"They are many," it reported.

"But," Anton said in Dalian, "I am a Brubiscon. I will not fail." Never had he felt so proud. Perhaps this was the world he was to conquer. The natives were bigger, but not smarter or wiser. He would succeed.

Thurgose activated the elevator.

~ * ~

"They're coming out," the aide told Alsop excitedly as the mechanism on the side of the spaceship moved.

Alsop put down his binoculars. "I want Canyon arrested the minute he steps into camp."

"Yes, sir."

"Bring the alien to me," Alsop finished. He walked back inside his tent. This would be a good setting. An alien and a general would meet. There would be a few pictures. And Canyon would vanish from history to be replaced by someone a bit more appropriate. Alsop sat down behind his desk and waited. He could see the figures nearing. There were two aliens and Canyon. Alsop reached into his desk and found a small flask of bourbon. He took a quick drink. Then he stared at the metal flask. *What could McCaulley possibly find in donuts?* he thought.

~ * ~

McCaulley read the text describing the capture of the alien and the arrest of Canyon. He closed off the tablet. "Next question?" he asked pleasantly, looking out into the bank of lights and the mingled maze of smiling faces. He could see the eagerness and fought back the desire to blurt the truth. There was a time to lie. He knew that fact very well.

He had learned it a long time ago on the Moon.

VIII

In the quiet of the corridor, Bonnie Cataline could hear her heart beating. She was sure that sound was being picked up on the special detection devices. Everything in this sunken, overly secret military base was recorded. For a moment, at least, she had to get away. Not that she could go far. Each tunnel led to another. Stretching endlessly, they seemed like giant worms that had swallowed everyone and everything. She felt her skin crawl as her claustrophobia worsened. She looked up. The white fiberglass ceiling was so low. The walls were hard, tile-covered; the floors, even harder concrete. She began to breathe hard. Stop it, she ordered herself and straightened up. She was not going to fail now. She certainly wasn't going to get out. The women's restroom was not that far away, and she stumbled to the door. Once inside, she sat down on a sofa. There was so much quiet. Canyon said over 10,000 people used to wander through this secret facility, checking on the equipment, keeping in computer contact with bases around the world. Now there were 500. None of them were allowed in this sector. They didn't know why. Cataline did. The alien Anton was being held here.

She knew where he was imprisoned. The room was large and decorated as he requested. She had helped. The young alien had been very friendly, practicing his English with her. He learned fast, but not fast enough. He thought the humans were going to help him rebuild his planet. Even Cataline had lied about that. Many times. That's how she got this far. She could still see Anton, looking eager and excited, as she told him they were now recruiting workers.

"When will I be able to address them?" he had asked. He had taken out his little stick and was waving it around. She never did learn its purpose, but supposed it was a baton or something similar.

"Soon," she had lied again. That was good enough. He was content to let the Americans examine his ship, question him, take his pulse, his picture, his temperature, his life history. He chatted happily for hours. His little mechanical horse would not leave him. General McCaulley said the horse should be disarmed. Cataline did not worry about McCaulley. He was nice, told jokes and made sure everyone had plenty of donuts.

On the other hand, General Alsop scared her. He would sit, staring straight ahead at staff meetings, his long, gray face growing even more solemn as time wore on. Nothing slipped by him. He was maintaining media contact, keeping up the glider façade. That had been damaged a little when an enterprising reporter hired a private plane and flew over the landing site. He saw the alien vessel, of course, the same one filmed and broadcast worldwide a few days earlier. However, Alsop said it was merely a transport to remove the glider.

When that explanation unraveled, since no transport landed upright, Alsop allowed himself to be "updated." It was, he said with grave assurance, a rocket being tested. He even smuggled in an Atlas rocket and ran a test for the media. At the same time, the thin, grim general had so reorganized this secret Wyoming facility that only the handful of the occupants knew about Anton. McCaulley probably didn't even know where Anton was being kept.

That was a worry, too. Cataline stayed up long hours in her small compartment wondering what Alsop would do with her after Anton had either died or been disposed of, after he had been drained of all his secrets. Alsop certainly wouldn't need her. She wasn't worried about Sinone. The Ethiopian was a competitor; he could fend for himself. And Canyon was not worth consideration. He had lynched himself with that one-man suicide mission. Alsop would have cashiered him weeks ago if Anton had not asked about Canyon and requested he be nearby. Dalians are loyal, he had said. Not that Anton necessarily liked Canyon, but he was the first representative the alien had met and was thus the most familiar.

Cataline took a deep breath and stood up. She wished she could spend a few hours on the surface and see the sky through something other than a television screen. No, Alsop said firmly. "That is not possible. No one who knows can leave." He issued that command as though he were pronouncing an epitaph. She shuddered as she thought about it. Perhaps he was.

She stepped into the hallway. Harsh sounds radiated towards her. Holding onto the door, she peered ahead as far as she could. Just shadows coming around the curve in the tunnel. Guards. They were everywhere. Brawny men all loyal to Alsop. He had his own little army here. The two soldiers marched past her without a glance. They frightened her, too. At times, she wondered how many bodies were buried in these walls. Maybe Anton's question about Wyoming wasn't that frivolous.

"How could any good come out of a place whose name starts with a question, has a groan in the middle and a grunt on the end?" He was serious. She had no answer.

Cataline began to march down the corridor away from the central hall. At an intersection of four tunnels, she read the signs. "Authorized Personnel Only." They were yellow and black. They were also electrified. She touched her I.D. card which she kept attached to her dark suit coat and walked on. The light in the center of the sign flashed red. An image was sent immediately to the monitoring station. She knew what that meant.

But she refused to stop.

What would Alsop say? He would fix his blue eyes on her, look through her, and ask for an explanation. She would reply, as planned, she thought she was scheduled for a meeting with Anton. At 4 p.m.? he would counter in that accusing tone. Her schedule was lost, and she was afraid she would miss her allotted visit. Afraid was the right word. Alsop was terrifying. He would not believe her. At that point, her years of work just to get this far would be gone. She was smarter than most people she knew. She had played the game well, but there was no future at the end of this.

Still, she could not leave Anton. That wasn't right. He was outside the game. Now he was playing, and he didn't even know it. He agreed to everything in the belief he would get what he wanted in return. Only Thurgose protected him. She was only going to make things fair. She was going to let him know.

There was a buzz next to her, and she almost jumped. The communications box blinked green. Hesitantly, she opened it and looked in. Alsop was looking back. She adjusted the viewer's focus so he was slightly distorted. He could see that, but did not comment. "Ms. Cataline," he said, "you are not carrying your cellphone."

"No, sir. It is in repairs."

"And, you are in a restricted area."

"I...," she fumbled. The words wouldn't come out right. "I must have taken the wrong tunnel. I get lost here so easily."

"Retrace to the exit, by following the black line on the side of the wall." With that, Alsop disconnected the circuit. She blinked for a moment and stepped back. She knew about colors. Every tunnel had one. It made getting lost very difficult. Her mind whirled. She could feel the cameras watching her. They were everywhere, too. These were not for the computers, but for security. There were no monitoring cameras here. Alsop wouldn't let them wire the cave. He did not care civilians were now inside—a first for the facility. He would elevate them. McCaulley had overruled that. Not the equipment. Just the rating. McCaulley would do that himself. Alsop had shrugged, and the matter was settled. She knew what her evaluation would say. She had disobeyed direct orders. Her rating was going to nosedive.

Maybe she would join Gerald as an Outsider. That was a strange thought. It jarred her just to think of her brother living in the desert, unkempt, unmotivated, a leech on society. What a strange time, too. Somewhere behind her, someone was watching her carefully, someone with a finger poised over an alarm button. And she was thinking of her brother who had become an Outsider. He would appreciate the irony. She had never been more regimented in her life. He had never been freer. That's all changing now; she thought as she warily eyed each communication box she passed. Everything was ending.

For a moment, that seemed funny, but she didn't laugh. Another thought kept intruding. It edged over the corner of her mind like the dark shadow of a cloud cutting a swath as it blocked the sun. She felt a tremor run through her. The communication box to her right buzzed urgently, but she ignored it and walked on. The sound from her high heels hitting the tile was loud, but it couldn't block the thought, the reason for her mission. Nothing would or could. She began to tremble. Her legs almost buckled; then, she righted herself. Her pace picked up as her face paled. Any moment, the alarms would sound. And they would keep on ringing until she was stopped. She dreaded that moment, but she did not hesitate. She couldn't.

She was going to free the alien.

The idea was so frightening. The first time she had resolved to do it, her courage had wavered too much. Courage was nothing more than manic tendencies taking over for a normal behavior. Wasn't that what scientists said? Brain synapses misfiring. She had read that somewhere. Standing in her room, staring at the wall, the concept had seemed funny and horrifying at the same time. But she knew she had to help him. Much of the preliminary work was easy. She simply walked in the wrong direction after leaving his room. The tunnel broke into three different openings. Two had colors; one did not. That meant it was a tunnel under construction. There might be no cameras down there. Better yet, there might be no way to trace anyone who went down that way. Certainly, there were not enough workers.

This was her third visit here. Each time, she memorized which tunnel to follow—the one on the left—and noted any landmarks she could see to help guide Anton. After each visit, she had returned to her office quickly. No one had said anything. If Alsop had been alerted by her behavior, he did not comment. Of course, he was like that. He would watch, silently planning how to eliminate any problem. She had sat in the next staff meeting, glancing at him every now and then. McCaulley talked; Alsop was quiet. Yet, he had seemed to stare right through her.

Her mind made up, she continued on. How far was Anton's room? She could almost hear the alarms going off in Alsop's office. He was watching her. She could feel his eyes on her back as she passed each closed-circuit camera. Staring, just staring. Her shoes were so loud, for a moment she considered removing them. She wouldn't be able to run in them. But she wouldn't be able to run anyway. Anton may be able to find his way through the maze and out. She was walking toward a dead end and she knew it. As her pulse quickened, she began to move even faster. She imagined soldiers grabbing their weapons and racing down the tunnel after her. There couldn't be that many, but one was more than she wanted to face.

Almost out of breath, she began to run. Her tight dress clung to her legs and forced her to sprint stiffly. She fought the cloth and her own emotion. She heard a noise and stopped. Buzzers were sounding behind her. Another corner turned. Another after that. The noise was fainter. Then, another, more eerie sound. Anton was singing in his native tongue. The words sounded harsh, guttural with the many clicks and smacks that accompanied Dalian speech. There was a guard in front of the solid metal door. The song was slipping through the space below the door. The guard turned to face her, gun on his shoulder.

"Hurry," she said, her voice catching on her breath, "open up."

"I need authorization," he said. There was no emotion.

"Can't you hear what's going on? I have to warn Anton," she cried loudly, hoping he would hear her. The singing continued without a pause.

"I need authorization," the guard repeated. His hands were white on the gun. Cataline noticed and she relaxed a minute. He was scared, too.

She gulped. "Look, you call your commander. I'll talk to Anton. That way we don't waste time."

"I'm not allowed to." His voice was edgy now. He was watching her carefully. *Just a boy*, she thought. *He doesn't know what to do.*

She moved closer. "Sergeant," she barked. "You know who I am and why I'm here. I didn't not have time to pick up a damn piece of blue paper. Now you contact your superior to see I'm all right. This is an emergency, and I won't waste any more time."

He licked his lips, half torn with indecision. Across the hall, the communications box blinked green and buzzed. It had a sound of urgency to it. "I need…," he started, then glanced at the box.

"Answer it," she ordered. "That's your proof."

He didn't move at first, then, finally, walked across the corridor. Behind him, Cataline reached into her purse. She knew it would come to this. He stiffened to attention on the phone. "Yes, sir," he reported as he listened. It was the last thing he said. She shot him through the back of the neck with a stunner. He collapsed instantaneously. His gun rolled away. She almost reached for it, but moved quickly to the door instead.

"Please open," she called. The song ended.

"Who are you?" Anton said.

"Elucidate your identity," Thurgose added.

Cataline did.

"Hurry," she insisted. There was no way to hide the panic in her voice now. An eternity passed before the iron bolt clicked. She stumbled inside. The bright colors almost blinded her. Anton had a red, blue, gold and orange carpet, which coupled with brilliant gold walls, a crimson ceiling and a silver canopy over his bed. The effect was always breathtaking, and Cataline had little to spare. Gasping, she slammed the door behind her. Thurgose rolled between her and the Frighem. Its head had turned a pale green.

Anton stood up. He had been lying on the bed. He had his stick in his right hand, as if it were a knife instead of a baton. "What is going on?" he asked.

"You must leave," Cataline told him. She wanted to pour out the whole story, but there wasn't time. How could she warn him of the lies, the treachery, the way he was being used, that he would die here. That Alsop had threatened each of those who knew. "No one must find out the alien ever landed," he had insisted. His face had been as awful as she had ever seen it. This was to be Anton's tomb. It wasn't right. Already, Alsop was being touted as the next military 3. Sinone had been promised a major promotion as had his aide. Cataline had been taken aside and assured her future was secure. They would learn the secrets of space travel from Anton. They would separate Thurgose from him and tie the little horse to a computer and drain it of its knowledge. There would be no religious uproar over the arrival of an alien. No way his presence could be used in the ratings debate. He would be a stepping stone to their glory. Cataline would have needed weeks to explain that. "You must go," she pleaded.

They did not move. Thurgose was bright green now. "You are less than comprehensible," it said.

"They are going to kill you," Cataline cried. Why couldn't they see?

"Who?" Anton asked. His voice betrayed his feelings.

"Alsop," Cataline said. She could almost hear the soldiers getting closer. "McCaulley, everyone. They're never going to let you out of here. You will die here. Don't you see that? Don't you understand?"

The horse seemed to hear her. "I had postulated such a theorem," it said.

~ * ~

Anton nodded. He should have guessed, too. Maybe he didn't want to. They were keeping him in this barred room to protect him, the general said. The hordes of people who wanted to hurt him—he never saw one. Just the general and a few others. He felt the skla stick in his hand. He was wrong not to stand up to them. He should have marched in and demanded as a Frighem, as a Brubiscon, that they stop delaying. Where were his workers? Logic, he told himself angrily. Be wary of the mewing tiger. It still has to eat: Brobatton, just 230 years ago. Still, there was another side. This woman was one of them. She was mewing, too. He let Thurgose evaluate her. Its senses were far more powerful than his vision. It could analyze her emotions and determine whether to believe them or not. The green color told Anton the horse was alert and ready.

~ * ~

"They're coming," Cataline cried.

Thurgose moved beside her so he could look outside. It rolled quietly across the carpet. The warning sirens had replaced the buzzers. Thurgose saw the fallen soldier across the hall and slid back. "Which departure route is optimum?" it asked.

Cataline wiped her forehead. Sweat cascaded down her face. Anton liked his room hot, and she was feeling suffocated. "Take the corridor away from the center. Follow the one on the left. The tunnel on the left," she managed.

"Come, Brubiscon," Thurgose said. "We must evacuate."

"Guards. There are guards," Cataline said weakly. She handed over the stunner to Anton. "Use this." He let it fall to the ground. "They'll shoot you."

He snapped his skla stick in the air. "I am ready for them."

"Now is the time," Thurgose insisted. It rolled to the door. The air was thick with alarms, bells, sirens. The communications box was green. Thurgose looked at it. It carefully aimed and fired. A light cut the wire through the solid wall, slicing easily into the tile like a surgeon's scalpel. The box went dead. Thurgose then rolled to face any oncoming soldiers.

Anton followed. He paused by the door. "Will you join us?" he asked.

Cataline shook her head. "I have no future. They can't do anything to me except keep me here." She closed her eyes then opened them quickly as an image of General Alsop appeared before her. She would not outlive him. He would see to that.

"Then come with us," Anton offered. "We will need help."

She studied him. There did not seem to be a good reason to refuse. She could stay and be entombed. She could go and be a renegade. The choices were equally bad. "I…," she started. Running feet interrupted her. Soldiers were coming. "Go, just go," she said. They must escape. She would not sacrifice everything for nothing.

"There is room," Anton said. He was listening to the footsteps thundering toward them, too. "Thurgose can protect both of us."

The horse had set itself to face whatever came. Anton and Cataline moved behind it and started walking. She glanced over. The alien was so small, yet he had an air of such strength which gave him such stature. She wished she had some of his self-assurance. *What now*, she thought. *Where am I going?*

They heard a loud blast. Cataline whirled. She could see the complete scene. Bodies of at least a dozen soldiers were flung against the walls. They fell over each other in heaps. Several were missing arms. A few seemed to be sleeping. The carnage was awful. Thurgose rolled toward them. Its head was a bright green, its eyes sunken deep into its plastic skull.

"Now is the time," it repeated. There was not a hint of emotion in its voice. Anton stared and then swallowed hard.

"I did not want this," he said softly.

Those words echoed behind them as they turned and ran into the corridor. They did not know where they were going. Nor did they know what they left behind. The sirens roared. Cameras watched. Recorders noted every step they made until they disappeared into the dark unlit tube that led to their future.

The saga continues

Time Warp Book 2

Anton, Bonnie and Thurgose find a haven with the Outsiders, people who have dropped out of society.

Betrayed, Anton and his companions are returning to captivity as Wyron begins his assault. Anton's ship is the only possible defense, so the Prince is sent off with an odd human crew to face his enemy.

That's when the trouble really starts.

Coming December 2015

About the Author

At age 7, Bill Lazarus decided to be a writer and has been writing ever since. Born in Portland, Me., he grew up in Akron, Ohio and has lived in Connecticut and now Daytona Beach, Florida. He holds a B.A. and an M.A. in journalism from Kent State (OH) University and an ABD in American Studies from Case Western Reserve (OH) University.

During his career, he has been a newspaper reporter, magazine writer/editor, advertising copywriter and writer/editor of NASCAR programs, among other jobs. He has won three international awards for stories and programs while working for International Speedway Corp. and was named 2000 Florida Feature Writer of the Year.

He has been published articles in hundreds of local, regional, state and national publications as well as novels and nonfiction books. This is his first science fiction book.

These days, along with his own compositions, he has been ghostwriting a variety of novels and nonfiction books for clients from around the world.

In recent years, Bill taught English classes at Embry-Riddle Aeronautical (FL) University until retiring in 2014. Previously, he taught at Kent State, Case Western Reserve, Cuyahoga (OH) Community College, the University of New Haven, Yale University and Daytona State (FL) College. A religious historian, he also teaches classes as part of Stetson (FL) University's Continuing Education Department.

More mind bending Science Fiction from WolfSinger Publications

Aqua Vitae – Therese Arkenberg

Jenes Inarya wants to experience everything. And quite frankly, she doesn't think she can live life to the fullest in the time she's been allotted. A search through lore and legend from the Eight Immortals of Chinese myth to the Garden of Eden finally leads her to what she seeks--across the galaxy, to the planet of Arak, which possesses an immortal ecosystem. By eating food prepared from the immortal plants of Arak, Jenes can alter her metabolism and gain eternal life. In her case, it's a cup of palm wine. A real aqua vitae.

But the prospect of eternal life quickly causes more problems than it solves.

Claire – Sally Kuntz

It was an open and shut case of someone's reckless actions that had killed his sister. Mark knows that, and he is going to expose the group responsible for the wild, headlong, daredevils they are. But Mark has a lot to learn; about the killer and about himself.

Mark arrives on Eire's moon with a complete set of beliefs: it hadn't been his sister's fault in any way, the person responsible for shooting down his sister's ship, the group the killer belongs to are reckless scum, and he will right the situation by exposing them in print. But the longer he stays the less his beliefs apply.

Remember Me to Paradise – Amy Benesch

A Shapeshifter from a planet known as Paradise, comes to Earth on a mission to rescue other Shapeshifters who may have become trapped in Earth shapes and are unable to return to their home planet.

During his time on Earth the Shapeshifter becomes a dog, a duck, a pigeon, a human male, and a human female. It is as a human female that Shapeshifter begins to forget its true identity. She goes to a therapist who urges her to write down her dreams.

Although her dreams terrify her (she can't understand why she dreams of flying and of making love to women), she keeps working to put the pieces of the puzzle together and recover her memory, although with each passing day she becomes more identified with her current shape and less likely to believe the truth of who she really is.

Schrodinger's Cat – Eileen Schuh

Chordelia, straddling two of the realities proposed in Everett's Many Worlds Theory of Quantum Physics, has no idea how distorted the line is between choice and fate.

In one of her worlds, Chorie's young daughter is dying—a drama that quickly contaminates her other, much rosier, reality. Before long, the emotional burden of dealing with two separate lives spawns heated legal battles, endangers her role as mother and wife, and causes people in both universes to judge her insane. As her lives begin to crumble, so does Chorie's heart and mind.

When Dr. Penny, a man with disturbing, murky, hypnotic eyes offers to rid her of the life that's causing so much pain, she must decide if she is willing to sacrifice the chance to be with her dying child for the chance to save her marriage and experience happiness.

She thinks she's planned it well—she's researched her choices, prepared herself for the consequences, put everything in place. She makes her decision. However….

Life, as it has the propensity to do, strikes back with the dark and unexpected.

Dispassionate Lies – Eileen Schuh

The year is 2035 and the world's emerging from a devastating economic collapse. Computer guru, Ladesque, finds her task of restoring the world's internet capabilities, dull until…

She's approached by Paul, an attractive FBI agent intent on recruiting her to an ultra-secret project. There's only one problem—the asexuality she was born with thirty-five years ago, vanishes and she's left struggling with the unfamiliar power of libido.

When everyone, from ungainly computer geek, Roach to handsome Paul, becomes appealing, Ladesque suspects the popular explanation for the female asexuality saddling her generation is a lie. Her suspicions increase when an encoded diary and whispered rumours link the affliction to conspiracy and murder. However, uncovering facts proves difficult in an age where hackers have corrupted all digital records.

Putting her quest on hold, she joins Paul's project where her uncertainties are quickly overshadowed by the explosive technology and high-tech challenges of her job. Then, she receives her final assignment. She can either expose her mind to the potentially lethal quantum computer for the sake of the world or be forever a watched woman.

She, alone, must assess the risk—a risk that just might reveal the truth about her past.

The Station – A. David Smith

The distant future. Humanity has reached the stars…and found no life. On a remote space station, lone crewman Lt. Robert Bradley awakens to starless space and complete darkness.

When he summons the courage to venture outside, Bradley becomes the first human to embark on humanity's greatest journey. He will develop a new understanding of the universe and witness the destinies of countless sentient life forms.

Check them out at www.wolfsingerpubs.com